JULIE BARDEN, DOCTOR'S WIFE

Julie Barden, Doctor's Wife

by

Audrie Manley-Tucker

Dales Large Print Books
Long Preston, North Yorkshire,
BD23 4ND, England.

British Library Cataloguing in Publication Data.

Manley-Tucker, Audrie
    Julie Barden, doctor's wife.

    A catalogue record of this book is
    available from the British Library

    ISBN   1-84262-135-1 pbk

First published in Great Britain in 1969 by Mills & Boon Ltd.

Copyright © Audrie Manley-Tucker 1969

Cover illustration © Ben Turner by arrangement with
P.W.A. International Ltd.

The moral right of the author has been asserted

Published in Large Print 2002 by arrangement with
Rupert Crew Limited

Dales Large Print is an imprint of Library Magna Books Ltd.

Printed and bound in Great Britain by
T.J. (International) Ltd., Cornwall, PL28 8RW

CHAPTER 1

'My word, Nurse, marriage suits you!' Mrs Dellar said approvingly.

I laughed and agreed wholeheartedly with her. I had been married to Dr David Pembury only a couple of months, and still, whenever I met any of my ex-patients, they called me 'Nurse.' I rather liked it; happy though I was with David, working as his surgery-nurse, I sometimes missed my district nurse round.

District nursing is one of the most rewarding jobs in the world, I think; not just going the rounds to give treatments, blanket-baths, injections, and a host of other things for which nurses are trained, but a feeling of satisfaction that came from entering into other people's lives when one entered their houses; listening to problems that sometimes had nothing to do with illness, and feeling an extra bonus of satisfaction, on top of one's nursing work, if one was able to solve their problems.

'You look really bonny,' Mrs Dellar added. 'Now then, Nurse, what is it you want me to do with all these pieces of felt and things you've brought? Some toys for Miss Verney's

Summer Fair? Well, it's a good cause, I suppose.'

'One of the best,' I told her. 'The money goes to a Comforts Fund and provides extras for needy old people, especially at Christmas.'

Miss Verney, the Superintendent of the Nurses' Home, had telephoned only a few days previously, asking if I could help. I had promised readily, knowing many nimble-fingered ex-patients with time on their hands who would be glad to do so.

'Make some of your dragons,' I suggested. 'Nurse Jessop was telling me about them the other day. Lovely scarlet felt dragons with blue teeth and green spines!'

'All right!' Mrs Dellar promised, pleased. 'I'll make one for *you,* as well, Nurse!'

'I'm going to ask Mrs Carroll to make some of her pretty knitted things. How is she, these days?'

Mrs Dellar knew what I meant; her next-door neighbour was a difficult woman, who had almost ruined her daughter's marriage by being possessive. I knew that daughter Ginny and her husband, Phil, were settling down, and solving their own problems – but I hadn't seen Ginny's mother for some time.

'She isn't too bad,' Mrs Dellar conceded. 'I went in and had a cup of tea with her the other day. It's a bit of a strain sometimes; if she can't find something to grumble about, she'll invent something. Still, she did say that Phil hadn't made a bad job of the garden, last time he came up and did it for her.'

That's progress! I thought happily. I drove home to David feeling very pleased with life; and to round my day nicely, I discovered that he was back early enough from his afternoon rounds for us to have tea together before he began evening surgery.

'And how's my gadabout wife?' he teased, as he kissed me.

'Gadabout, indeed!' I pretended to be furious, and told him what I had been doing. The approval on his face set the seal of perfection on my day.

Dear David! It didn't seem possible that I had ever hated him! Our first meeting had been disastrous because I had quarrelled with him, believing that he could have done more for one of his elderly patients whom I was nursing – an unwanted old lady in very unhappy circumstances. Since then, when I had grown to respect and like him before falling in love with him, I never forgot the valuable lesson he had taught me: one cannot always do big, spectacular things for people, but the small daily services we give can be a great comfort to people who have little else.

David cupped my chin in his hand, and lifted my face to his, looking at me thoughtfully.

'Do you miss your patients, darling?'

'Sometimes,' I admitted frankly. 'I like an excuse to see them again, such as I have now. I still feel interested in them, and their lives.'

'Being my surgery nurse isn't quite the same for you, I know,' he said. 'No chance for you to have a chat with *my* patients about their troubles!'

'That's because you have so many patients!' I teased. 'Your surgery is always so full, you must be the most popular doctor in Ambersea! Now I suppose you'll have a swelled head!'

He laughed and kissed me, and I clung tightly to him for a moment. David was the last person in the world who would ever suffer from *that* particular complaint! I reflected happily.

The June afternoon was warm enough for us to have tea on the terrace. Afterwards, I put on my white overall, ready for my evening's work. David was a very busy doctor; he had a young receptionist who came in two or three times a week to help with the clerical side of the patients' records and catch up on the typing of reports and letters.

I was surprised to see Louise Whittaker in the surgery that evening. She was a pleasant, still pretty woman in her fifties, and her mother, a patient of mine during my district nurse days, had died suddenly while I was on my honeymoon. I had liked old Mrs Whittaker, in spite of her razor-sharp tongue; the beautifully embroidered cloth on which I had set out this afternoon's tea for David and myself had been her wedding present to me.

Louise, I knew, had taken her mother's death philosophically. The old lady was in her eighties and had been bed-ridden and in pain for years. I remembered the remark Louise had made to me, the last time I had visited the old lady.

'Sometimes I've regretted not marrying. People often remark that I shall be very lonely when I no longer have Mother to look after – but no, I've got a big house here. I shall let it into flatlets for students. That way, I shall always have young company!'

Louise had done that, so I had heard, taking in three or four young women from the local college. I remember thinking, when she had told me what she intended to do, that she had learnt the secret of contentment: adapting oneself to circumstances, instead of trying to make them fit one's own wishes.

Louise had arrived late, and was the last patient to see David. When she came out of his consulting room, I thought she looked restless, somehow; as though she had lost the secret of contentment, after all. But she smiled when she saw me, and said frankly:

13

'How are you, Nurse? Of course, it's Mrs Pembury now, isn't it? I can't think of you as anything except Nurse Barden.'

'I'm fine, Louise. How are you?'

She hesitated; there was an odd look in her eyes – as though she wanted to ask me something and thought better of it before the words were formed.

'Doctor has given me a prescription for a tonic. I'm feeling a bit under the weather – old age, I expect!'

Somehow, the joke didn't quite come off; I said briskly:

'Nonsense! We all feel that way at times! Even the nineteen-year-olds sometimes complain of feeling ninety! You're sure you aren't working too hard, though?'

She shook her head.

'There isn't anything to do. The girls keep their own rooms clean. They're lively company and sometimes they come and have a cup of coffee with me. I've started a new venture, Nurse. I used to be quite a good shorthand-typist, believe it or not – so I'm setting up in business at home, taking in typing and clerical work.'

'The best of luck to you!' I told her. She looked pleased, and asked me to look in and see her, any time I had ten minutes to spare.

I promised that I would; well, she isn't lonely, I thought. She has plenty to do, and she has company. Yet she had that air of being vaguely dissatisfied and out of tune with life. I told David about it, and he teased me.

'That's Nurse Julie Barden wanting to put the world right for everyone! Don't look at me like that – you know I love you for it, even though you can't hope to win all the time! Honestly, darling, I think Louise is just feeling a bit off-colour as a result of her mother's death, the rearranging of her life, and all the work she's had getting the house ready for the students, as well as starting up a typing business. Louise may be vigorous and a hard worker, but she's probably overdoing things a little.'

David talked common sense; yet I couldn't agree with his diagnosis, though I didn't tell him so.

I was too busy, during the next couple of weeks, to take up Louise's invitation to call and see her. Then, one day, I visited the Allisons – my ex-problem family. I had a very soft spot for seventeen-year-old Shirley, who had looked after her father and four younger brothers and sisters since her mother had gone away with a man 'friend.'

Shirley made me welcome, bustled around getting a cup of tea.

'I've come to see if you have any old toys that Paul and Heather and Lorraine have outgrown,' I told her. 'If they're in fairly good condition I can get them renovated to look like new; we're having a toy stall at Miss Verney's Summer Fair.'

Shirley nodded.

'It will do those kids good to turn out their toybox; they've got far too many toys,' she said, with the brisk, maternal air that always amused me. 'Of course, I'll have to get them used to the idea – kids hate parting with their toys. Could you come back in a few days – or maybe I could send Sandy down with them?'

'No, I'll collect them; that will be easier for you, as I have the car to put them in. How is Sandra getting on these days?'

'Doing very well at school,' Shirley told me, still with that as-one-mother-to-another air. 'She's been learning typing for the last three months, and she likes it. Do you know what she did? Saw an advertisement in the evening paper for a part-time typist – somebody who runs a typing office, down by the Pier.'

'Miss Whittaker?' I suggested.

'That's it. Well, anyway, Sandy never said a word to me, but she went along and said she'd do some typing evenings, for the experience and to get some extra pocket-money. Miss Whittaker said she wasn't old enough yet, but if she liked to come back when she left school, there might be a job going. I must say Sandy's got some nerve, hasn't she?'

I agreed. I was thinking about Louise as I left the Allison house, and decided I'd go and see her, though it would mean skipping tea.

As I reached the big house near the sea, Louise was just seeing someone out; a tall, good-looking man about her own age, with silver hair. It was a very friendly farewell. Louise waved to him as he got into a sedate-looking black car and drove away.

I closed the door of my own car behind me, and walked over to Louise; she was flushed and smiling.

'Business seems to be good!' I said lightly.

'Oh, that wasn't a client, Nurse! A friend of mine, John Wilmore. We knew each other years ago, and lost touch. He has owned a bookshop in Mallington – that's only a dozen miles inland from here – for years, and I haven't known! He saw the announcement of Mother's death in the paper and he's been writing to me. I didn't expect him to come over today, though we certainly had plenty to talk about!'

I couldn't resist asking:

'Is he a bachelor?'

'Widower. His wife died last year.' Her voice was suddenly brisk. 'Come and see my office, Nurse.'

She had turned the largest of the downstairs rooms into an 'office' and it looked very impressive with its desk and typewriter.

Louise told me she had received many enquiries and quite an amount of work in response to her announcement in the paper that she ran a typing bureau. She also told me about Sandy's visit, and I shared her amusement and appreciation of the enterprise of Shirley's fourteen-year-old sister.

That evening, over a late meal, I told David about Louise's visitor.

'I smell romance!' I told him happily. 'Louise needs a husband to look after – someone to make a fuss of; she's just the type to enjoy being married!'

'Now, Julie,' David said, gently warning, 'leave things alone, and don't meddle!'

'Who said I was going to meddle?' I demanded innocently.

'Ah, I know that particular look in your eye! You'd love to get an invitation to the wedding – then you would feel that all Louise's problems were happily settled, when, in fact, they might just be beginning.'

'Pessimist!' I retorted indignantly. 'I'm not *going* to meddle! I just thought how wonderful it would be for Louise – she needs someone to look after *her*, too! Anyway, they say only happily married people play Cupid!'

David had his usual answer for me. He laughed and kissed me, and I thought: he doesn't realise that I'm so happy with him, I'd like to see Louise happy with someone.

'I'll bet they're just good friends, anyway!' David teased.

I was delighted when I saw Louise, a few days later, going into a restaurant with John Wilmore, around lunchtime. Casually, I walked past the restaurant, a few moments later. They didn't see me; they had a window-table, and they were deep in conversation. Louise looked relaxed and was wearing a remarkably pretty hat.

I told David about it, that evening.

'Maybe you are right,' he admitted. 'I still can't see Louise settling for matrimony in a hurry, when she's just rearranged her life.'

I went to Louise's house a couple of days later, with the very valid excuse that I was counting on her to help with one of the stalls at the Summer Fair. She promised to do so with an enthusiasm that surprised me.

'Didn't I see you going into the Rendezvous for lunch a few days ago, with your friend?' I asked casually.

'Oh yes!' she smiled. 'John took some time off; he says he's worked hard at the book-selling business all his life, and now that he's got a good manager, he's going to relax. We're going to the concert at the Guildhall tomorrow evening – and I have a stack of typing to do first. Oh, it's good to be busy!' She added eagerly: 'Is there anything else I can do towards the Fair, Nurse? Something I can make or give? It's such a good cause. I suppose you came across a lot of old people who hadn't much, or hadn't anyone to bother with them, when you were district nursing...'

Her interest was a cover, I decided; she didn't want to talk too much about John Wilmore – well, I could understand that! It was her brand-new romance, perhaps the first real one in her life, and she wasn't prepared to discuss it – yet.

'These toys you're collecting,' Louise added. 'Who is going to renovate them?'

'We've got a team of volunteers!' I told her.

'I'd like to help there.'

'Louise, you're doing too much,' I said worriedly. 'With your students, and the typing, you already have your hands full!'

'I like being busy!' she told me again. I looked at her. She seemed to have shed twenty years, with such a brightness in her eyes and a glow in her cheeks. Romance was certainly a better tonic for her than anything David could prescribe!

I collected a pile of toys from Shirley, a few days later, and took some of them to Louise; I let Sandy come with me, as a treat. She thoroughly enjoyed the feeling of import-ance it gave her. Sandy was a nice child, bright and cheerful, and one day she was going to be attractive.

Louise was delighted to see us. John Wilmore was there, and she introduced him.

'I'd like to help towards the Fair, Mrs Pembury,' he told me. 'Would a present of half a dozen children's books from my shop help your cause?'

'Indeed it would!' I assured him joyfully. I liked him immediately! He was kind, pleasant, really interested in what we were doing – and it was obvious, from the way he looked at Louise, that he adored her. I could *smell* orange blossom in that room!

Louise let Sandy type out a list of the toys I had brought; it wasn't really necessary, but I realised she wanted to give her something to do. I watched Sandy, laboriously typing, and saw Louise's smile. Louise was fond of children; a pity she would never have any of her own. She had shown great interest in the Allison family when I had told her a little about them, and expressed her willingness to help in any way she could.

'I envy you, Nurse,' she said, unexpectedly. 'You have had so much opportunity to do things, really important things, for people. I wish I was young enough to train as a district nurse. I like this business well enough, but it isn't the same at all!'

Louise wouldn't need to worry about nursing or running a business much longer! I reflected. Not with such an attentive suitor on hand!

I saw Louise and John together several

times, after that. David asked me how the romance was progressing.

'I'm getting impatient!' I told him frankly.

'Well, Louise hasn't been back for a repeat prescription of the tonic, so she must be feeling better,' he told me with a gaily impudent smile. 'Don't think you can hurry Cupid, my love. Look what a long time it took us to get together!'

'Still, I think I'll invite them along to dinner one evening next week,' I told him. 'Give them both an opportunity of seeing how attractive domestic bliss can be!'

As it happened, I was kept too busy to see Louise for almost a fortnight. And then, one morning, on my way to Miss Verney with some letters and reports from David, I saw Louise sitting alone, drinking coffee, in the Copper Bowl. She had a forlorn look about her, and my heart sank. I hadn't time to stop; the traffic lights changed to green, and I drove on, still feeling uneasy about that solitary figure.

It turned out to be a bad day for me. In the afternoon, I went to Mrs Dellar's to collect the toys she had made. As I reached her front gate, Ginny, Mrs Carroll's daughter, dashed out of the house next door, looking white and worried.

'Oh, Nurse, could you come...? I was just going to ring for the doctor – it's Mum! I think she's had a heart attack!' she told me.

I was Nurse Barden again, not Mrs David Pembury. I went swiftly into the house, Ginny following. Mrs Carroll's bed was still downstairs in the front room, although she was up and about most days. Now she lay on the bed, her face grey and drawn, one hand pressed against her chest as though it hurt.

I propped Mrs Carroll up against the pillows, put a blanket over her, felt for her pulse. Ginny was right; it was a heart attack, and I sent her out to telephone her mother's doctor.

Fortunately, Dr Paice was still having a late lunch when Ginny telephoned; he came immediately and confirmed that it was a heart attack. He left a prescription for Ginny to take to the chemist.

'It's a painful heart condition more than a serious one,' he told me. 'She has probably been overdoing things a little. I'll look in tomorrow. Is she living alone here, Nurse?'

I smiled. Like everyone else, he still thought of me as Nurse Barden!

'Yes – but her daughter can probably stay for a day or two,' I told him.

I had a shock when Ginny returned with the prescription.

'I'll be staying,' she told me curtly. 'I've left Phil; *really* for good, this time!'

'What went wrong?' I asked, dismayed.

'Oh, Phil wants everything *his* way! He

won't listen to me. There was this job, you see; it's a much better one than he's got now, more money and everything. A friend told me about it; but Phil won't hear of it – says he's rather stay in a safe job, one he's sure of! But that's only part of it...'

Listening to Ginny's breathless voice, I glanced at Mrs Carroll. She would be glad to have Ginny home again, I thought bitterly. She had always been possessive, and never approved of Ginny's marriage; yet, looking at her, I was puzzled. Her head was turned away, her eyes were closed, and she looked weary; it was more than just a recent heart attack, I thought. If I hadn't known better, I would have sworn that Mrs Carroll was none too glad to see her daughter back!

Ginny's angry tirade came to an end at last. She looked at me as though expecting me to say something, and seemed quite deflated when I didn't answer; but if she's counting on me for sympathy, or expecting a mini-lecture on the perils of matrimony, she's going to be unlucky! I thought grimly. I felt tired, and – for once – unable to cope. I was still worrying about Louise – quite unnecessarily, probably, I decided.

'Thank you for coming in, Nurse,' Mrs Carroll said quietly. At one time, I thought, she would have been rude and ungracious about my presence in her house.

I collected the toys from Mrs Dellar, who promised to look in and see Mrs Carroll later that evening. I decided I *had* to go and see Louise. I drove away, feeling thoroughly depressed at the thought of Ginny's broken marriage.

Louse was in her office, typing busily. She took off her glasses when she saw me, and plugged in the electric kettle to make tea. She rubbed her eyes and I thought how tired and dispirited she looked, but she asked how the plans for the Summer Fair were going. I told her about the soft toys Mrs Dellar had made, and how Mrs Dellar lived alone; how she had wanted children and grandchildren.

'There must be a lot of people like that,' Louise said slowly.

'Indeed there are; people to whom a visit, someone to drop in for a chat or a cup of tea, would mean so much. Not only old people, either; there are younger ones, housebound through illness. It's a long, long list; sometimes the daily visits of the district nurse are all they have to look forward to...'

Silently she made the tea. Something really *was* wrong, I thought uneasily.

'I called to see if you and Mr Wilmore would have dinner with David and me next Thursday evening,' I said.

'I'm sorry to disappoint you,' Louise said calmly, 'but I won't be seeing Mr Wilmore again. He's selling up the business and retiring to the country somewhere. Cornwall, he said; he has a married sister living there.'

I felt as though the bottom had dropped out of my world.

'Oh no!' I said aghast. 'You two were such good friends!' I went blundering on, desperately wanting to put things right. 'I was so pleased about you and Mr Wilmore! All these years you've looked after your mother, and now you're on our own; you seemed so happy together, so right for one another. What happened? Don't you want to go to Cornwall? Did you quarrel...?'

Of course, they were questions I had no right to ask, and Louise answered me with understandable exasperation.

'No, we didn't quarrel, Nurse. John wanted to marry me, and I didn't want to marry him, that's all. Don't look so astounded! I'm not so desperately unhappy living on my own that I want marriage at any price!' Her voice was as sharp as her mother's had once been. 'There's nothing wrong with turning down a proposal of marriage to someone with whom you are not in love; or do you imagine that any marriage is better than none? *I* don't! I'm not in love with John, and love is the only reason for considering marriage. *That* isn't what's bothering me.'

I didn't dare ask her what *was* bothering

her; she looked angry and tearful and embarrassed, all at once. I drank my tea and made my escape. For once, I thought ironically, I hadn't honoured my own code of helping people when they needed it. Louise obviously had something on her mind, but I felt, literally, too exhausted to cope.

Even so, the wretched day wasn't quite over. Driving home, I caught sight of Phil, Ginny's husband, staring aimlessly into a shop window. On the pretext of getting some cigarettes for David, I left the car at the kerb, and walked across. I wasn't going to help, I thought angrily. Whatever I did seemed to go wrong; it was just that the sight of that hunched, forlorn figure made me feel guilty, in some way; probably because I had rejected Louise by my silence, I felt I should make it up to someone else – and here was Phil.

'Hello, Phil!' I said.

He turned and half-smiled; his face looked white and strained.

'Ginny's left me again,' he said baldly.

'I know. I heard about it today. I'm sorry.'

'She was so set on me taking this new job with a car-hire firm. But they aren't sound, and I tried to tell her so; she wouldn't listen. She's been so irritable and funny lately. Oh well, I suppose her mother will be pleased to have her back!'

'I'm not so sure of that,' I said slowly. I drew a deep breath and added, out of my own experience:

'There's a time in life for doing nothing, saying nothing, Phil. Just waiting and letting events shape themselves. If I were you, I wouldn't run after Ginny. Just go home and wait for her to come back.'

'And if she doesn't come?' he asked.

'I think she will,' I said, with more conviction than I felt. I was a hopeless failure, I thought dismally. I wasn't really able to help anyone at all, and, for the first time in my life, I felt too despondent to try.

Somehow I got through evening surgery. When the door closed behind the last patient, I sat down in the waiting-room, and burst into tears.

David led me firmly away, into the seclusion of our own room, and sat me down in his chair.

'Now,' he said briskly, 'there's been something wrong with you the whole evening – I've seen it and I haven't been able to say anything, with a stream of patients coming and going. All right, my love; what's wrong? Start at the beginning, and let's have a nice clear statement so that I can make a proper diagnosis...'

I couldn't even raise a smile at his touch of humour. It all tumbled out in a muddled confusion of words, about Ginny and Phil

28

and Louise, and my bitter disappointment over the broken romance.

David put his arms around me and held me tight.

'Darling,' he said, with his quiet common sense, 'you're disappointed because Louise isn't going to get married, but *Louise* isn't suffering from a broken heart. She's right, you know; marriage for love is the only worthwhile kind – *we* should know that!' he whispered against my hair. 'Why don't you try to find out what's really bothering Louise and see if there's something we can do? As for Ginny and Phil – well, anyone who tries to patch up a marriage feels the way you do sometimes: everything seems to be going well, then it comes unstuck again. You did all you could; and it's up to them now. You *tried*, Julie. That's all anyone can do. You cared enough to want to help – that's the most important thing of all. The failure isn't in *you*...'

I leant against him, feeling his strength and needing it as I had never done before. David could smooth away the rough places, reduce my mountains of disappointment and despair to the molehills they really were, David could make my world right and he was the centrepiece of that world; I loved him so very much.

He held me without speaking for a long time. Finally, he said briskly:

'Doctor's prescription! Dinner at the Bay Hotel. I'll ring and book a table for two. remember, it was there that I tried to propose to you, when all the lights in the place suddenly went out...?'

Do you wonder that I love him?

I called on Mrs Carroll a few days later, to see how she was. Ginny was out shopping. Mrs Carroll gave me a couple of very pretty tea-cosies she had knitted for the Fair.

I didn't mention Ginny until I was leaving; then I said casually:

'So Ginny's back with you for good?'

'So she says!' Mrs Carroll retorted bluntly.

'You aren't pleased!' I said blankly.

Mrs Carroll shrugged.

'I never approved of the marriage. He hasn't enough go in him, though he treats her well enough. But *she* married him and she can't expect to come running home, upsetting my life, every time they have a quarrel...'

Would I ever understand human nature? I wondered, bewildered, as I drove away. Once, Mrs Carroll had welcomed her daughter home triumphantly; but now the old lady had begun to make another life for herself, a pleasant little routine of tea and chats and visits next door – and Mrs Dellar had told me she had even persuaded Mrs Carroll to come shopping, once or twice.

Mrs Carroll didn't want a daughter coming home with her troubles, upsetting her tranquillity...

I shook my head and laughed; one day I should probably grow as philosophical as David. And it was no use fretting any longer over their broken marriage; better to accept that some things just couldn't come right.

I went to Louise, straight from Mrs Carroll; she had just finished work on a pile of manuscript. I marched in and sat on the edge of her desk, coming straight to the point.

'All right, Louise!' I said. 'So you haven't got a broken heart. What *is* worrying you?'

She sat back in her chair, and said unhappily:

'It will sound too silly for words!'

'Try me!' I invited gently.

'Well,' she drew a deep breath, fiddling with her glasses, 'I've got the students and I can take in as much or as little typing as I please. I've got enough to live on very comfortably. And I'm not doing anything *useful!*' She banged her fist down on the desk. 'You were lucky, Nurse! You could do things for people! Little things, maybe, but important. I'd like to have been a probation officer, a nurse, anything that would have brought me into contact with people who need someone to help them over a tough patch. But how can I find them? Where do I

31

look for them? I haven't got any qualifications, any Social Science degrees; but I'd love to do things for people who haven't anyone to help them, to be necessary...!'

I heard the yearning in her voice. Oh, I had been blind, I thought, beginning to understand. She had wanted to renovate the toys, been so eager to help with the Fair, she had shown tremendous interest in Sandy, knowing the child's background. It all added up.

I smiled at her.

'Louise,' I said, 'only this morning, Miss Verney told me they were looking for someone to help with the hospital library, taking the books round the wards. The woman who has been doing it for years is giving up. Then there's Malcolm Anderson, the probation officer – you've never met him, have you? He's a friend of David's and one of the nicest people I know. Go and see him and tell him exactly what you've just told me, and I guarantee he'll come up with some names for you! And I've my own personal list I'll supply you with on request! Old people who'd like someone to look in for tea and gossip, people who want someone to shop for them – or just someone to *be* there and make things seem a little less lonely and difficult for a while. That's the kind of job you want, isn't it?'

'Please!' said Louise eagerly. 'Oh, bless

you, Julie! I could start tomorrow, if you'd give me that list!'

She looked like a young girl, I thought wryly. Love had never made her look like that! I had forgotten that after years of knowing she was useful to her mother, Louise would miss that awareness of being needed; marriage could never have given it to her half so fully. Cupid had let me down badly!

I went home in quite a subdued frame of mind, and told David about it.

'I shall never understand about human nature, darling!' I told him.

'But you'll go on trying,' he pointed out. 'That's all we're meant to do, I believe. Never mind – maybe you're a shocking failure as Cupid, but as Mrs David Pembury you're a big success!'

I felt a lot better for his testimonial!

Oh yes, I almost forgot – a couple of evenings later I saw an announcement in the evening paper that the firm Ginny had wanted Phil to work for had gone bankrupt. I hoped Phil would have the sense not to say 'I told you so'– if he ever got the chance to say anything to Ginny, I thought.

I met him about a month later. Someone touched my arm as I was leaving Carmichael's, and there he was, smiling at me.

'Nurse,' he said confidently, 'I thought you'd like to know I took your advice and

33

waited for Ginny to come home. It worked! She came back after she read in the paper that the firm she wanted me to work for had gone bust. And it's going to be all right this time. After all, if you're going to be parents, you have to stick together, for the sake of the baby. Ginny's expecting, Nurse, just before Christmas. No wonder she was so irritable and strange ... and her mum's thrilled to bits about being a grandma. You'd think *she* was having the baby...!'

I went home light-heartedly. It sounded like the traditional happy ending, but I was growing older and wiser, and knew life didn't offer such simple solutions to its many problems. Ginny and Phil would have their ups and downs, maybe they would even part again; perhaps they would never make it in the end. I just hoped they would. Go on trying, David had said.

Suddenly, I wanted David more than anything in the world; I wanted to be with him, hear his voice, savour all the joy of my happy marriage over the afternoon tea break we always shared.

I got in the car and drove home to David as fast as the speed limit would let me.

CHAPTER 2

'It's going to be a fine day!' I said, as I pulled back the curtains. 'Thank heavens! Rain would have spoiled everything!'

'What's so special about today?' David murmured sleepily. 'It isn't our wedding anniversary or anything, is it?'

I laughed at him. Sitting up in bed, with his dark hair tousled, my husband looked more like a schoolboy than one of Ambersea's most successful young doctors.

'No, we still have to wait a few months for our first anniversary,' I reminded him. 'It's Miss Verney's Summer Fair at the Nurses' Home – remember? She's having it later than usual this year, but early September is quite nice, I think – and it's going to be hot. You'll look in this afternoon, if you possibly can, won't you, darling?'

'Of course.' He put out a hand, and pulled me down beside him. 'I might even buy you something. That's very noble of me, seeing that I have to eat my lunch out because you'll be working there all day.'

'You know perfectly well you don't mind!' I retorted. 'The money we raise goes towards Miss Verney's fund to provide comforts for old people at Christmas; and if you don't get up, you'll be late for morning surgery!'

I went happily downstairs to cook David's breakfast. I was looking forward to helping at the Fair, which was being held in the big, tree-shaded grounds of the Nurses' Home. Many people who had been my patients in the days when I was a district nurse had made soft toys and other articles to be sold.

Getting these things made and collected had given me opportunities to visit my ex-patients that I welcomed. Happy though I was as David's wife and surgery nurse, sometimes I missed the very personal contact with people that is part of a district nurse's life.

Sally Allister called for me promptly at ten o'clock. Until last Easter she had been Sally Carmichael, and her father owned the town's largest department store. She was a happy, warm-hearted person, and today there seemed to be a special glow about her, as she stepped from her car wearing stretch pants and silk shirt.

'This is my working rig,' she explained. 'I promised Miss Verney a couple of hours help getting the stalls ready. Then I'll have to dash home and robe myself in my best dress and put on a *hat* ready for the opening this afternoon. I've never taken kindly to hats.' She looked at me quizzically, and added:

'We have a very well-stocked maternity department at Carmichael's. I must pay it a visit some time soon!'

The announcement was typical of Sally; it was a few seconds before I understood.

'Sally, I'm so thrilled!' I told her delightedly. 'When will it be?'

'Next spring. In time for our first anniversary, I think.'

I knew David would be pleased. A thought drifted through my mind, light as thistledown, a half-expressed wish ... well, there was time enough yet, I reminded myself; but David and I wanted children. My own particular and unexpressed wish was for a son like David...

The grounds of the Home were looking their best, the borders still bright with summer flowers, no sign of autumn amongst the trees that opened green umbrellas above the smooth lawns.

Miss Verney asked me if I would take charge of the soft toy stall. Many of the toys had been made by Mrs Dellar, a one-time patient of mine who lived in Poplar Street, and had a surprisingly fanciful imagination when it came to designing toys: there were dragons in brilliant coloured felt, bright green frogs with yellow ears, fat cheerful pigs covered with polka dots and many other fantasy creatures, making my stall as bright as a rainbow. Sally, who was arranging 'flowers and potted plants', wandered over, and fell in love with a scarlet-spotted pig.

'I'll buy it for you,' I promised her, with a smile. 'And when you're tired of playing with it, you can put it away for Junior-to-be!'

'You know who's opening the Fair?' Sally asked, as we downed tools for a cup of coffee.

'Yes. Delia Fairfield.'

We were both remembering. Delia had not been a patient of mine – her husband was Arnold Fairfield, owner of the local paper, and if *she* had been ill, Delia would have been a private nursing home case; but she had collapsed one day at Carmichael's and been taken to the sick room; I had been at the store at the time, and Sally had asked for my help.

I had discovered that Delia was taking slimming tablets, and her collapse had been due to skipping meals. She had accepted our attentions very ungraciously, but it was impossible not to feel deep pity for this handsome, middle-aged woman, who was obviously unhappy. I had learnt that her marriage was childless, and that her husband was having an affair with his secretary, a young woman in her twenties. I suspected that Delia had been making frantic attempts to shed years and inches in the hope of making herself glamorous and winning back her erring husband.

I just had time to dash home and change into my best suit before Delia arrived, promptly at two-thirty, to open the Fair. She looked magnificent – tall, well-built, elegant in an expensive hat of lacy black straw and a suit of tawny silk. Few women of Delia's age would have been able to wear such an outfit, but she carried herself with a poise through which none of her unhappiness showed. Only her eyes betrayed her.

There was at times a flicker of interest in those lovely eyes, as Delia approached my stall. She was intrigued by the collection of animals, especially the ones Mrs Dellar had made.

'These are most unusual!' Diamonds sparkled icily in the afternoon sunlight as an exquisitely manicured finger stroked the spines on a dragon, touched the ear of a cherubically-smiling pig. 'I've never seen such fascinating toys. Who made them?'

'Mrs Dellar. She was a patient of mine when I was district nurse,' I explained. 'She tells me that she would much rather make extraordinary animals than ordinary ones!'

Delia Fairfield looked thoughtful.

'Would it be possible for me to purchase a reasonably large quantity of such toys before Christmas?' she asked. 'I should very much like to take them to the Children's Home on Christmas Eve. I know that the younger children will love them.'

'I'm quite sure that Mrs Dellar would make them for you,' I told Delia Fairfield enthusiastically.

Delia nodded, and discussed details in a businesslike manner. I was to purchase the materials on her account and Mrs Dellar was to charge for her work.

Mrs Dellar would find the extra money very useful, I knew. Best of all would be her own personal feeling of usefulness, so very necessary to older people, who live alone, have no family and feel that they have no real part in the business of living.

During a brief tea-break, I told Sally about it.

'I had no idea that Delia Fairfield was interested in the local Children's Home,' I said.

'Oh yes. She's on all kinds of committees and things for welfare and social work in the town, but I suspect it's just a "filler" for long, empty days. With the Children's Home it's different, somehow,' Sally said thoughtfully. 'She's really keen on this; she pays for all of them to see Father Christmas at our store every year, and buys toys and games, as well as providing the tree. Looking at her, one wouldn't imagine she cared. Her husband may be disappointed that he hasn't a son to carry on the newspaper after him, but I think Delia is equally frustrated and unhappy that she never had children.'

'As they both shared the same disappointment, I would have thought it would have brought them closer together,' I told Sally.

'So would I. My father says Arnold has always been rather gay, though. He's in his fifties, a very charming and handsome man; but I think it's all wrong that he should flaunt his affair with his secretary right under Delia's nose. Doug and I saw Arnold with Elisabeth – his secretary – having dinner in the Fig Tree the other evening. Oh, she's a pretty little creature, slim and dark, and she was flattering Arnold, making a huge fuss of him!' Sally's voice was disgusted. 'I hear he gives her expensive presents and takes her out a great deal.'

'I wonder why the Fairfields never adopted a child?' I mused, and Sally shook her head.

I had a few nice surprises that afternoon. The first was David, walking across to my stall, just after four o'clock. He picked up a bright green frog, and said:

'I thought this might keep my younger patients amused while they're in the surgery; what do you think, Mrs Pembury?'

'A good idea,' I said demurely. 'We only have two frogs left. Why not buy the other one as a gift for your wife, Dr Pembury?'

41

'You think she'd like that?'

'I'm sure of it,' I told him. We laughed together, and seeing the tenderness in his eyes, I thought fleetingly of Delia, reminding myself how lucky I was to be married to David.

I told him Sally's news. His eyebrows rose and he looked pleased.

'That's fine!' Deliberately he leant across and said softly:

'Our turn next, darling!'

The Thorpes paid me a visit – I was surprised and delighted to see them; it was many months since I had attended Mr Thorpe. This elderly couple had been trying to manage on a shoestring income and had been too proud to seek any financial help. I had been instrumental in getting Mr Thorpe a job as Father Christmas at Carmichael's, and I had always felt a tremendous sense of satisfaction about this, especially as Sally found work for him at the store after Christmas was over.

Mrs Thorpe was wearing a pretty hat and a flowered dress, and smiling happily when she saw me.

'How are you, Nurse?' (So many people still called me that!)

'Fine!' I told her. 'No need to ask how you both are! Are you going to be Carmichael's Father Christmas again this year, Mr Thorpe?'

'I certainly am! I'm looking forward to it!'
He smiled at his wife, and inspected my toys
before he added casually:

'We're looking for a present for my
grandson.'

I looked astonished, remembering the one
son in Australia with whom the Thorpes had
no contact. I had been told that there had
been a family quarrel long ago.

Mrs Thorpe glanced at her husband, and
said:

'I wrote to Geoffrey – our son – just after
last Christmas,' she explained. 'I sent him a
photograph of his father, in his Father
Christmas outfit. Geoffrey wrote back, and
we've been writing ever since. He's married
to an Australian girl, and their little boy is
two. He says he's coming home to England
one day, so that we can see our grandson.'

I heard the lilt of pride in her voice, and I
was so happy that I wanted to cry. I did not
know what had caused the rift between the
two generations of Thorpes and I probably
never would; it was enough to know that the
gap was closing. I couldn't help feeling that
the Thorpes' improved financial position
had something to do with the letter they had
written to their son; they had been too proud
before, too afraid he would guess their circumstances and think they wanted help...

I sold a rabbit and an elephant to the
Thorpes, thinking what a lovely day it was,

and how wonderful that some of life's true stories had the happy ending one usually finds in fiction!

I was packing up the stall as Shirley Allison dashed past; she was wearing a very short skirt, and her red hair was flying like a brief, bright banner.

'Hello, Nurse! Look!' She smiled rather sheepishly and held out a book I recognised. It was a collection of fairy tales, part of a consignment of toys Shirley had given me for the Fair.

'I bought it back!' she explained, seeing my puzzled look. 'Gosh, I was lucky to get it! I couldn't get down here early, and I thought it would be sold.'

'Don't tell me you've started to ready fairy tales, Shirley!' I teased.

'Not *me!* I like a good romance!' she replied with a worldly air. 'This was Lorraine's. I told her she was getting too old for fairytales – and that she ought to give it away. She didn't say much, but I found the silly kid crying her eyes out the other day. Said she liked her fairy tales and wanted the book back. I didn't tell her I was coming down today to buy it, in case I was unlucky. I bet she'll be tickled to death when I give it to her! Imagine all that fuss over a book! Aren't kids *funny*, Nurse?'

'Very,' I agreed gravely. 'But it was a kind thing for you to do, Shirley.'

She scuttled away, embarrassed and pleased.

I was tired, when Sally finally dropped me at home. Evening surgery was over. The warmth of the day lingered in the comfortable, old-fashioned house.

David was waiting for me. Without a word, he sat me in a chair, and took off my shoes.

'I'll bring you in a cup of tea in two minutes,' he promised.

I looked at the twin frogs sitting on either side of the hearth. I looked at David and said blissfully:

'I *do* love you!'

He paused at the doorway. His eyes were wicked, but his voice was matter-of-fact.

'Cupboard love! Just because you need a cup of strong tea, and I can make it better than anyone else you know!' he retorted.

It was a few days before I could collect the material Mrs Dellar needed for making the toys. A couple of days after the Fair I went up to town to have lunch with my old friend, Sister Clare Martin, with whom I had trained. She was still at St Christopher's, still seeing Alan Roberts, my journalist friend from Ambersea whom I had met the day I started district nursing – and with whom I had once believed myself in love. Now I had hopes for Alan and Clare; but Clare, guessing by my discreet questions over lunch, laughed and shook her head.

'Stop it, Julie! Alan and I are the best of friends, that's all! When I fall in love, it will be suddenly, head over heels, and I shall *know*, directly I meet him…!'

'Nonsense!' I said firmly. 'I loathed David when I first met him! I thought he was rude and arrogant and callous. It was ages before we even became friends.'

Clare laughed, and said:

'You know the old saying about hatred being akin to love! Tell me all about your patients, Julie – or I should say "ex"-patients. I enjoy hearing about them.' She was quiet for a moment, before she added calmly:

'I have news for you, Julie. I'm going to train for district nursing. You loved it so much, because of the personal contact side of it – and I think I'd like that, too. I've been happy enough at St Christopher's, but the time has come to make a change. I'd like to work in a town like Ambersea.'

I was delighted. Clare would make a wonderful district nurse, I thought happily, as I went home to David that evening.

A couple of days later I took a collection of materials and odds and ends to Mrs Dellar and explained what Mrs Fairfield wanted; Mrs Dellar was delighted at the prospect of creating toys for the Children's Home. Her pleasure gave me an idea that I tucked away out of sight until the time came for me to see Delia Fairfield again.

Mrs Dellar worked hard and by early October, she had produced several toys for me to take to Mrs Fairfield.

'They're marvellous!' I told Mrs Dellar happily. 'You could make a fortune if you went into business!'

I meant it. She shook her head, laughed, and said she was too old to bother, but the glow of quiet pride on her face warmed me against the sharp little wind blowing down the last of the pale leaves, as I drove to the Fairfield house.

It was big and imposing, a detached house in well-tended grounds in the most exclusive part of Ambersea. I had telephoned to tell Delia Fairfield that I was coming, and she answered the door to me, ushering me into a hall elegant with expensive flowers, Chinese rugs, lovely old copper.

The drawing-room into which she took me was even more elegant, the furniture old and beautiful; and yet, I thought, as I sat in one of the pale green brocade chairs, it was an empty sort of luxury. This wasn't a living, breathing house; it was a background for two people with money, and I could not imagine laughter, untidiness and all the small, happy things of family life being part of this house.

Two paper-thin cups and saucers were set on a silver tray. Delia lit the flame under a small spirit kettle.

'You'll have a cup of tea?' she said with formal courtesy; but even Delia thawed a little when she saw the toys.'

'These are beautifully made – and such imagination. The children will love them!' she said.

I talked to her about Mrs Dellar.

'She lives alone; she's a cheerful, happy person – but lonely. She is a widow, and misses never having had children or grand-children,' I said.

I saw what could have been a flicker of pain in Delia's eyes. Mrs Dellar had few of this world's goods, Delia had an abundance – but neither of them had the one thing they really wanted.

'I'll write her a note of thanks,' Delia murmured.

'She'd like that,' I said appreciatively. I hesitated. This was the moment to tell Mrs Fairfield my idea.

'I believe there's a scheme for Children's Homes and such places whereby people – particularly those who have no children – can "adopt" a child, taking the child out, remembering birthdays, taking an interest in it,' I said; and when Mrs Fairfield nodded, I added:

'Wouldn't it be possible for Mrs Dellar to

be a kind of "adopted grandmother" to a child from the Home? I know she would love that.'

'Adopted grandmother?' Delia looked intrigued. 'An excellent idea! Of course, it rests entirely with the people who run the Home, but I'll mention it to Matron, Mrs Pembury, and I'm sure she'll be agreeable.'

'I won't say anything to Mrs Dellar until it's all settled,' I said.

I watched Delia, busy with the kettle. She poured tea into the shallow, beautiful cups and asked me polite social questions about myself and about David's work; and all the time, the loneliness that she could not hide showed through her words, in her voice, her face.

Only once that afternoon did Delia show any real animation; that was when she mentioned to me, casually, that her sister-in-law Helen, Arnold's only sister, was coming to stay. Helen was a widow with one son, Peter, at University.

'They're coming for Peter's half-term holiday,' Delia explained. There was brightness in her face, softness in her cool, clear voice, as she added:

'Peter is Helen's pride and joy.' *And yours, too,* I thought, with sudden understanding. 'He is in his first year at University, and has ambitions to be a writer. The house always seems so full of life when he is here. He's intelligent, and good company – and thoughtful. So many young people, these days, are careless and thoughtless, Mrs Pembury ... but not Peter.'

She talked for some time about Peter, reminiscing about the holidays he had spent at the Fairfield house when he was a boy. Her laughter had an almost robust sound to it when she recounted to me some of his youthful escapades.

Nevertheless, I was glad to get back to my own home, to the companionableness of David, and the joy of our shared life together. David and I were so lucky to share work, as well as play. I felt strongly that if Delia could have shared her husband's work, it would have compensated a great deal for her childlessness.

As it happened, I saw Arnold Fairfield, the following day – going into the town's leading jeweller's with his secretary clinging to his arm. He was certainly very good-looking, with an air of maturity, and self-assurance that would have tremendous appeal for a younger woman. And Elisabeth, his secretary, was half his age – hard and smart. I didn't like her. It was obvious Arnold was shopping in the jeweller's for something Elisabeth wanted. Had he no love or concern for his wife? I wondered, puzzled. Where had their marriage gone awry?

I had news of the Fairfields again some days later – in a tragic and most unexpected way.

It was a wild, wet afternoon, the day dying stormily, gusts of wind tugging at the bare tree branches. David was late back from his afternoon rounds, but this was not altogether unexpected, considering the long list of patients he had to visit.

I put on my white overall, fretting that he would scarcely have time for a cup of tea before evening surgery, and I breathed a sigh of relief when finally I saw his car pull up outside the house.

When he came in, I saw that his hands were dirty; there was blood on his coat, his hair was awry, the knees of his trousers muddy.

'David, what's happened?' I asked sharply.

'Julie, I need a wash. Run some hot water for me, there's a good girl.' He came across and looked down sombrely at me. His face was strained, his eyes looked bleak.

'There was an accident,' he said briefly, 'on the new bypass. Three cars in a pile-up. I haven't any details yet – I just happened to be on the scene, a minute after it happened. Arnold Fairfield was driving one of the cars. He's badly hurt and liable to be in hospital for some time.'

'Delia?' I asked quietly.

'Shocked, cuts and bruises, but that's all.

There were two other people in the car – a youngster of about nineteen or twenty. He was thrown clear, and there isn't much wrong with him; but there was another, older woman, sitting next to Arnold. She's dead. There was nothing I could do for her.'

I put my arms tightly around David for a moment, trying to shut out the distress, the remembered horror, I could hear in his voice. Doctors and nurses become accustomed to injury and death, but there is something particularly dreadful about a car accident; perhaps because of its suddenness, its unexpectedness.

'Two people were hurt in the second car,' David added. 'The man in the third car seemed to be all right. I don't know who the people were with the Fairfields.'

I could guess; a youngster of about nineteen – that would be Peter. And the woman? Peter's mother, probably, though I hoped I was wrong.

I lay awake that night, thinking about the accident, whilst the wind buffeted the house and drove the rain in sharp, angry gusts against the windows. Poor Delia! Money could not cushion her against unhappiness – money could never do that for anyone. I reached out for David's hand, in the darkness, counting my blessings.

There was an account of the accident in the local paper the following evening.

Arnold had not been the guilty driver; the man in the third car had been going too fast on a wet road, and had skidded. Arnold Fairfield was seriously ill in hospital, and the dead woman was Mrs Helen Duncan, Mr Fairfield's sister. Mrs Fairfield and her nephew, Mr Peter Duncan, had escaped with superficial injuries.

I thought a great deal about the Fairfields during the next few weeks. Sally Allister brought me some surprising news of them one afternoon. Her father, who owned Carmichael's, was a business acquaintance of Arnold's.

'Arnold is going to be in hospital for some time,' Sally told me. 'But Father says that Delia has been down to the newspaper office a few times; and there's no sign of Elisabeth, Arnold's secretary. She seems to have disappeared.'

I called on Mrs Dellar the following afternoon. When she opened the door to me, she looked as though she was over-flowing with happiness.

'I'm a grandmother, Nurse!' she said joyfully.

I chuckled.

'Don't tell all your neighbours, just like that, will you?' I said. 'You'll give them such a shock!'

She took me into her little sitting-room.

'It's you I have to thank, isn't it? There was

53

a letter from Mrs Fairfield, thanking me for the toys, and then a few days ago, she wrote saying there was a little girl at the Home who would like a grandmother, and if I liked the idea I was to get in touch with Matron. She said you suggested it to her…'

So Delia hadn't forgotten her promise, in spite of her own heavy load of sorrow and trouble, I thought.

Mrs Dellar had the rest of the toys ready for me, and I decided, suddenly, to deliver them in person, though I had hesitated to call at a time when the Fairfields probably did not want visitors; but I wanted to thank her personally for the joy that old Mrs Dellar was feeling.

It was a little over a month since the accident, when I rang the bell of the Fairfield house with some misgivings, especially as I had not telephoned Delia, telling her that I was coming.

I did not quite know what to expect when Delia answered the door; certainly not a briskly capable woman, her grey hair a little untidy and looking as though it needed setting. She had none of her usual flawless make-up – just a touch of powder and lipstick. Funnily enough, instead of making her look older, it stripped years from her age.

'Mrs Pembury! Do come in!' A voice that I remembered as politely social, was warm and welcoming.

Feeling dazed, I followed her into the long drawing-room; there was a subtle feeling of change here, too. It wasn't immaculately tidy. There were papers spread over a table, as though Delia had been at work. There were some books in a corner, a man's leather glove on the window-ledge, the cushions seemed *rumpled!* It was incredible – this air of warmth, of cosy, family disorder. Delia's transformation was the most surprising thing of all.

'Thank you for bringing the rest of the toys,' she said sincerely.

'Thank *you* for what you've done for Mrs Dellar,' I replied, and told her how Mrs Dellar had greeted me, how happy she seemed.

Delia's pleasure was a tangible thing; it gave me courage to say frankly:

'I didn't know whether to call or not. You've had such an unhappy time.'

'Yes,' she admitted candidly. I saw pain and distress in her face for a moment; but no bitterness, I realised, such as there had once been. *This* was a clean wound whose edges time would close together.

'It was fortunate for Arnold that your husband was on the spot,' Delia added quietly. 'Arnold will still be in hospital for some weeks yet, but the doctors tell me he should make a complete recovery. Helen's death, of course, was a great shock. Especially to Peter, naturally.' She hesitated, and then told me:

'The young are resilient, Mrs Pembury. Peter has taken it remarkably well. We're his only relatives now, and he will make his home with us in future. Arnold is pleased about that. He always wanted a son, you know, and it will make a difference to us both, having young company here at holiday times.'

She looked happy. She looked, too, as though she wanted someone to share that happiness with her, so there was none of her usual reserve about her.

'Peter wants to be a writer. What better apprenticeship could there be than working on a provincial newspaper? Arnold is very keen to have Peter on the staff when he leaves University, and the idea seems to appeal to Peter,' Delia added.

'And you?' Her lack of reserve made me feel less constrained with her. 'You look as though you're busy – and liking it!' I told her.

'I am! Someone must keep an eye on things at the office. I go there each day, and I give Arnold progress reports! He's very pleased with me!' Her voice and face were like a young girl's. 'I tell him he's certainly not going to have me sitting in the background when he's better. I think I surprised him, Mrs Pembury; he has never expected me to be efficient in business. This after-noon, he told me he would see about employing me permanently, if I could produce references! That's the first time I've seen him really smile since the accident.'

There was a moment's silence, before she said:

'Things are a little disorganized at the moment, as Arnold's secretary left rather suddenly. I'm looking for a good secretary. If you hear of someone suitable, do let me know!'

'I will indeed!' I promised her gravely.

I counted my blessings all the way home. I thought of the big house and the woman who ran it – both of them alive for the first time in years. I was growing old enough and wise enough to know that life never produces tidy answers to problems – Delia and Arnold probably had plenty ahead of them still; but I had the feeling that life was going to give them both a second chance, and that they would be taking it with both hands, especially as Arnold seemed to have discovered he had a wife worth more than second place in his life.

I kept my fingers crossed for the Fairfields, beginning to make the long, slow journey back to one another. My own marriage gave me a rich glow of contentment! Life was good, I reflected thankfully, as I put the car away.

CHAPTER 3

The red-haired girl sitting in David's surgery reminded me of Shirley Allison; but seventeen-year-old Shirley had a happy-go-lucky disposition that showed in her pert, pretty face. This girl was sullen-looking.

I sighed. It was going to be a busy evening for David, after an exacting day. Not that he ever complained; he loved his work, and it was a great joy to me that I could share in it.

'You're going to be busy tonight,' I told David, as I made a last-minute check that everything in his consulting room was ready for him.

He smiled and ruffled my hair lightly.

'When am I ever anything else?' he teased.

'Do you mind, darling? Do you sometimes wish you weren't a hard-pressed G.P. but a consultant, with inches of thick carpet under your feet and nice leisurely hours?'

'No!' he replied firmly. 'I like life just the way it is. Not that consultants have it all that easy, either!'

He kissed me and laughed; David was never too busy for tenderness, and it was one of the nicest things about him, I thought contentedly.

58

'All right, Julie. I'm ready for the first patient!' he told me.

The surgery was full. I thought longingly of the quiet meal David and I planned by the fireside and reflected thankfully that at least he wasn't on call this evening. Late call duty was shared out between all the doctors in Ambersea, which certainly made life easier for us all.

At last all the patients had gone – except the red-haired girl. She stood up languidly when I called her name. She wore a smart, tight green dress and jacket to match. Her heels were so high that I wondered how she walked on them.

I looked at the record card. Mrs Carol Palmer aged twenty-three. I had been a nurse long enough to make my own deductions, before David called me into his consulting-room.

'I want to examine Mrs Palmer, Nurse,' he said.

Carol Palmer submitted to the examination with an air of bored indifference. Being a district nurse teaches one to be observant about people. I noticed the expensive little gold wristwatch she wore, the thick mascara on the spiky lashes, the smell of good perfume.

David finished his examination, and Carol dressed again. I looked at the pretty, sullen little face while David told her what she wanted to know – and I wasn't altogether surprised at the reaction. She looked angry, trapped and resentful.

'Most women are pleased at the idea of having a baby,' David said to me, when at last we were enjoying our leisurely fireside meal. 'If she wasn't married, I could understand it; and this is her first.'

'Perhaps it isn't her husband's,' I said quietly. 'There is that possibility, David. She hasn't been in Ambersea very long, has she? According to her records, she was a patient of Dr Harmond at Mallington – that's some way from here. It's rather sad that she obviously hates the idea of having a baby.'

'Well, whether she likes it or not, there's nothing she can do about it,' David replied crisply.

I forgot about Carol during the next few days. I was busy getting ready for the Summer Fair.

I remembered her, suddenly, a couple of weeks after the Fair was over. I had called on Mrs Dellar, an ex-patient of mine, to see what progress she was making with the toys that had been ordered by Delia Fairfield.

I walked to Mrs Dellar's, because it was such a lovely day. On my way back, coming along the High Street, I saw little Miss McCade stepping briskly in my direction. Laura McCade had been a dressmaker since her retirement from Carmichael's, the town's biggest department store, where she had been alteration hand.

'Hello, Nurse Barden – I mean Mrs Pembury!' she said cheerfully. 'How are you?'

'Fine!' I smiled at the cheery little woman who had made my wedding dress so exquisitely. 'No need to ask how *you* are! You're looking very well; and business is good, judging by the dress box you're carrying!'

'Oh, it certainly is!' she agreed. 'This is a party dress wanted in a hurry. I saw Miss Carmichael yesterday – well, of course, she's Mrs Allister now!' Laura, who had a very soft spot for her attractive young employer, smiled conspiratorially at me. 'Have you heard her news? I'm sure you must have, as you two are such friends. She's going to have a baby in the spring. I'll be busy doing some sewing, I can see! Of course her father will miss her help in running the store, but I'm sure he'll be a proud grandfather!'

Yes, Sally was thrilled, as well I knew. I had shared her joy in the news; and David had said to me: 'Our turn next, darling!' I hoped so much that he was right.

Yet Carol Palmer had no welcome at all for the baby she was going to have. Fate played stupid practical jokes at times, I thought.

The arm of coincidence is longer than

most people think. I called at Carmichael's a few afternoons later, to do some shopping, and decided to spend five minutes with Sally before I left.

She was working in her office, but she pushed her papers aside, delighted to see me.

'Hello, Julie! Doug has just telephoned and said we're going out tonight to celebrate being parents-to-be because we won't be able to celebrate on the night the baby is born, he said! Isn't he sweet and crazy? Stay and have a cup of tea with me.'

We had tea and a leisurely chat before it was time for me to get ready for David's evening surgery. As Sally was showing me out, I saw a figure I recognised come from the main office farther along the corridor, papers in hand. She walked to the Accounts office, without seeing either of us.

'Carol Palmer!' I said, surprised.

'Do you know her?' Sally asked.

'Patient of David's,' I said.

Sally didn't ask questions. She knew that I could never discuss with anyone except David what happened behind the doors of his consulting room.

'Actually, I'm a bit bothered about her,' Sally admitted. 'She seems under the weather. Mrs Vesey, our Welfare officers, suggested to Carol that she should see the doctor and get a tonic, but Carol snapped her head off. Carol is married, and all Mrs Vesey can gather is that she came to Ambersea when her marriage broke up a couple of months ago; she's only been with us a few weeks. She told Mrs Vesey this morning that she had to leave her digs and was looking for somewhere to stay. Mrs Vesey promised to do what she could. *I* feel Carol shouldn't be in a place entirely on her own. Any suggestions?'

'Louise Whittaker has a room to let,' I told Sally. 'One of her students left at the end of the summer term. Louise is a nice, motherly soul and would see that Carol isn't alone too much. I'll have a word with her and let you know.'

I went to see Louise the following day, and she readily agreed to take her in. There was a big, bright room vacant, on the first floor.

'Is she a lame duck, Julie?' Louise asked me bluntly.

'Yes; her marriage has broken up,' I said. 'I don't know much more than that. She works in Carmichael's office.'

Louise's eyes were sharper, her perceptions more acute, than I had realised. She came to dinner with us, one evening the following week.

'How is Carol Palmer settling in?' I asked.

'She's difficult – not a person one would get to know easily, though I keep trying. She seems to have a huge chip on her shoulder.

Don't look so worried, I like a problem I can get my teeth into! She's pregnant, isn't she?'

Louise said it so calmly that I looked at her in open-mouth astonishment.

'How did you know? Did she tell you?'

'No; I've got eyes, and even if I haven't had any children of my own, I'm fifty-five, not fifteen! One gets a feeling about these things!' Louise retorted.

David looked amused. I explained to Louise that it had been impossible for me to reveal such details about a patient of David's.

'Don't worry about that!' Louise said. 'I'd still have taken her, anyway. She's terribly unhappy and hates talking to anyone. I'm not giving up yet.'

Dear Louise! She was a wonderful person, I thought. Carol Palmer didn't know how lucky she was!

By mid-October, it was obvious that Carol Palmer was pregnant; she was so unwell at the office one afternoon that Mrs Vesey sent her home, having first confided her suspicions to Sally, who tackled Carol as soon as she returned to work.

'She implied that it was no business of mine that she was having a baby,' Sally told me wryly. 'I don't know the story behind it all, Julie, but it doesn't seem a particularly happy one, and she doesn't want this baby. I'm so lucky, aren't I...? Anyway, I told her she could stay on in the office here as long as she felt able to. She seems to have no family or friends, and when I mentioned her husband she simply froze up.'

Both Louise and I also worried about Carol's lack of any contacts. Louise could get nothing out of her at all. David had made arrangements for Carol to attend ante-natal clinic, but she did not do so.

I saw Carol one morning when I called on Louise. I opened the front door, stepped into the hall and was about to knock on the door of Louise's office, when I saw Carol coming down the stairs, elaborately dressed and made up.

'She's out,' Carol said ungraciously. 'She won't be back until lunch-time, so she said.'

'It doesn't matter – nothing important,' I said cheerfully. 'How are you keeping?'

She looked hard at me, frowned and said:

'You're the nurse at Dr Pembury's surgery, aren't you?'

'Yes. I'm Mrs Pembury,' I told her.

'Then I suppose that's how everyone knew I was going to have a baby!' she said rudely.

I was angry for a moment; but anger melted. She was a scared child, underneath, I thought.

'Don't you know that neither a nurse nor a doctor's wife ever discusses what happens in their surgery?' I said pleasantly. 'I told no one. I don't think the ante-natal clinic would approve of stilt heels, do you?'

'Nothing to do with them what I wear! Besides, I haven't got time to go to the clinic, with all those mums getting together for knitting and cosy chats!' Her voice was scornful.

'I thought you worked at Carmichael's; have you left?' I asked her.

'No. I didn't feel well, so I took the day off. Anything else you want to know?'

I said nothing. She was rude, but it was the rudeness of the young, the defiance of the lost and lonely, I thought. She walked past me, head in the air, leaving behind a drift of expensive perfume. I remembered the watch, the good clothes. It was clear that Carol Palmer had been used to having money.

At the door she turned, looked back, and said – for all the world like a child wanting to shock its elders:

'I couldn't care less if I didn't have this baby, after all! In fact, nothing would please me better!'

I repeated the conversation to David.

'It's time she stopped thinking about herself!' he said shortly.

Carol came to morning surgery, a couple of days later. I thought how ill and grey she looked. Hardly had I admitted her to David's consulting room than she collapsed. We got her on to the examination couch.

With the colour gone from her face, she looked pathetically young and tired. I felt a stab of pity for her; but when she came round, David told her curtly if she didn't take care, she would lose the baby.

'That would suit me fine!' she retorted.

David was furious with her. I knew he was longing to say a good many things, but the moral issues were not his concern, as he pointed out to me afterwards.

A couple of nights later David had to go away to a medical conference. We had not often been parted during the few months of our marriage, and the house seemed terribly empty without him.

At ten o'clock, the telephone rang. The call was from Louise, and she sounded frantically worried.

'Julie? It's Carol Palmer. She took an overdose of aspirin – little *idiot*...!'

'All right,' I said quickly, 'I'll come over! Do you know what to do?'

'Yes; keep her awake. I've got her in my office here now.'

When I arrived, Louise was grimly walking a furious, protesting Carol up and down the office. I made some hot, strong coffee. Carol, in her dressing-gown, no make-up on her bitter little face, was hating us both with furious venom.

'Why can't you leave me alone! I'm sick of people trying to help, telling me I ought to be pleased about the baby! I don't *want* it! I don't even want to go on living...!'

She began to cry angrily.

'Carol,' I said firmly, 'you realise this will have to be reported. Dr Pembury is away, but Dr Paice is on call tonight. I shall have to ring him, and he'll probably decide you have to go to hospital.'

'Oh, sure, tell everybody!' she cried furiously. 'And there'll be a charge, won't there? What business is it of *anyone's* what I choose to do? It's my life...'

'You're not the only one concerned!' Louise told her sharply. 'You have the baby to think of as well – whether you want it or not, you're going to have one!'

'Not if I can help it! I'd have got rid of it long ago, when I first knew, if I'd had the nerve!'

'Why?' I asked bluntly. 'Because it isn't your husband's?'

'That's my affair!' She jerked away. 'I'm sick of people like you and Miss Whittaker. I just want to be left alone – *can't* you understand that?' Her voice slurred, her eyelids were heavy. We kept her walking while she protested wildly. She pulled away, overturning a chair. She was no calmer by the time Dr Paice had arrived. He sent for the ambulance, and while we waited, Louise and I told him what had happened.

When finally Carol had been taken away,

Louise asked:

'*Will* there be a charge, Julie?'

'She'll probably get probation. And it will be a good thing for her to be under the supervision of a woman probation officer. You can't cope with her on your own, Louise; don't look like that – you haven't failed! We don't know enough to be able to help her as she needs to be helped!'

'She's just a kid, really,' Louise said. 'A silly, scared kid, who's terrified of having this baby.'

I was right. Carol was in hospital only a couple of days, was charged with attempted suicide when she came out, and was put on probation. The Probation Officer, Miss Kenway, wouldn't have an easy time with her, I reflected. Joan Kenway was a nice woman and I knew her slightly, as she was a friend of Nurse Barbara Connolly, whom I had known in my district nurse days.

Carol did not go back to Carmichael's to work. Louise told me she had offered Carol part-time typing work – and to her surprise and delight, Carol had accepted, though with a great show of indifference.

'I hardly ever see her,' Louise told me. 'She keeps to her room, even does the typing there. Her work is very good, but she seems more sullen and withdrawn than ever.'

David and I were both kept busy with an influenza epidemic in the town, so it was a little while before I saw Louise again. She had been kept busy, she told me, for so many offices had depleted staffs due to illness that they had been glad to give her typing and clerical work to do.

I called, unexpectedly, one afternoon, and went into Louise's office. Louise wasn't there, but Carol was putting a finished pile of typing on Louise's desk.

It was the first time I had seen Carol since the night she had taken the overdose; she was wearing a maternity smock, and her awkward little figure aroused sudden pity in me. Her hair needed setting, her face was puffy as though she had been crying, and her look for me was hostile.

'Miss Whittaker has gone out to deliver some work,' she said curtly.

'Do you know when she'll be back?'

'About twenty minutes; she said you were to wait in here for her. Do you want some tea – there's some made,' she added ungraciously.

'I'd love a cup,' I told her.

She poured out without a word. As she passed me the cup, she said contemptuously:

'I suppose I've got you to thank for the fact that I have to trot down to the Probation Office once a week, and put up with

70

Miss Kenway coming here to see me when she feels like it?'

Suddenly, my patience snapped.

'I *had* to report you! I have a duty to my husband and to my own profession. You're utterly selfish, wallowing in your own misery, instead of thinking of the baby you're going to have – a baby that doesn't *ask* to be born, remember! Miss Whittaker has tried to help, so has Mrs Allister, so have I! We're all getting tired of your tantrums, your complete indifference to anyone but yourself. A fine mother *you'll* make! Do you imagine you're the only woman who was ever expecting a baby she didn't want? It's about time you grew up and learned to make the best of it! Most women do!'

I shouldn't have said it, I thought miserably; such an outburst was undignified, and would do nothing to help the situation.

But I was wrong – as I so often am where people's reactions are concerned – for Carol, after a look of fury and resentment, sat down in the nearest chair and burst into tears. Louise said she never cried. I had the feeling that this spate of tears would heal, in some way.

'You don't understand!' she wept. 'All right, so this isn't my husband's – I left him two years ago. I was only seventeen when I married Alec. Oh yes, he was a nice, decent, steady fellow! Not the sort to set the

71

Thames on fire! It got dull, I was so bored, *bored* with it all, and Alec didn't want me to go out to work. Then I met Mark...'

'And he was exciting?' I said gently, beginning to see daylight at the end of the long, dark tunnel.

'Sure, he was exciting!' There was a world of bitterness in her desolate voice. 'He had a flat in the new block that had just been built near Raynton Park. He had some kind of job with a jeweller's, and he knew how to live – parties, people, everything *I* wanted from life. Good times and plenty of money!'

'So you went to live with him?'

'Yes. I left Alec. Oh, it was wonderful at first. It was *real* living – plenty of company, and Mark liked to be going somewhere, doing something, all the time. *You'd* have enjoyed it if you'd been cooped up in a dreary little semi-detached, all day, with no one to talk to, only a lot of dull neighbours with kids. Alec was quite content to come home at night and potter about in his workshop, or the garden. Mark knew how to give a girl a good time!'

'What went wrong?' I asked. 'Wouldn't Alec give you a divorce?'

Her smile held a world of misery and disillusionment.

'Mark didn't want to get married! Oh no! The only kind of wedding rings he was interested in were those his firm sold. He got fed-up with me – I suppose you're going to say I told you so! Why don't you?'

'Because it's the silliest, most unhelpful expression in the world!' I replied calmly. 'So Mark got tired of you?'

'Yes, that's just about it; he got fed-up with me – after eighteen months, he was all set for somebody fresh. He got himself into debt, gambling, and he took all the money I had. When the money ran out, he told me to get out, and go back to Alec. It wasn't until after I came here that I discovered I was going to have Mark's baby! *Now* do you understand – I don't want a child with a father like Mark Roberts!'

'The baby isn't going to grow up to be a gambler, and a no-good!' I replied firmly. 'Children are largely what parents make them. I think you should try to get in touch with your husband – if he's the decent, steady sort, as you say, he may be only too glad to have you back.'

She shook her head. In spite of her tear-blotched face, her voice had a dignity I had not suspected she possessed.

'No. I won't do that to Alec. He'd take me and the baby and never say a word, but it wouldn't be fair, after what I've done to him.'

I knew it was no use arguing with her. She went out of the room without another word. She seemed spent and exhausted, but I

73

knew there was nothing I could say to comfort her.

I felt so dreadfully sorry for her. Life was so easy, so pleasant for me, I thought soberly. Carol Palmer had been guilty of a foolish mistake, but plenty of people made mistakes and were punished far less severely; she needed her husband, and I felt he would be kind to her, but I knew it was impossible to persuade her to go back to him.

When Louise returned, I told her all that Carol had told me. Louise sighed and shook her head.

'Carol is the type who will insist on going through with it alone,' she said.

Talking about what had happened seemed to make some difference to Carol; she could still be sullen and uncommunicative, rude and ungracious, but there was a faint suggestion of a thaw, a response to Louise's kindness, that was small but encouraging.

Louise decided to stay at home for Christmas; two of the students had parents living abroad, and she wanted to 'make Christmas for them' as she put it; she was also determined that Carol should have a good Christmas.

And after it happened, Louise insisted sadly that she would always blame herself for the accident...

It was the second week in December.

74

Louise had planned a frieze of holly and ivy around the picture rail in the hall. Surprisingly Carol had offered to help; I watched her climb the step-ladder, as I went into Louise's office, and automatically, I said:

'Be careful, Carol!'

'I'm all right!' she retorted ungraciously. She was looking tired and drawn and even the pretty maternity smock that she had reluctantly accepted from Louise could not hide the fact that she was six months pregnant.

'How did you enjoy your trip to Mallington with David?' Louise asked me, as we went into the office. She put three cups on the tray, took out a tin of biscuits.

'Fine!' I said briefly. I was just a little bit on edge. David's suggestion, the previous day, that I should accompany him to Mallington where he was visiting a colleague had come out of the blue. The idea had taken shape in my mind, as we drove there; after all, Carol herself had supplied me with the information that Mark Roberts lived in the new block of flats near Raynton Park. There would be a porter or caretaker; it was obvious that she would have lived there with Mark as 'Mrs Roberts' and the faintest possible chance that there might be a clue that could lead me to Alec.

I only had two hours to myself before David collected me. I didn't tell him what I was going to do, because I knew that he would have said I was meddling in other people's lives – and he would have been right – but sometimes I have hunches that I have to follow; often they are wrong – this time, I was lucky. The porter at the block of flats told me that a Mr Alec Palmer had enquired some time ago about 'Mrs Roberts' and left his address and telephone number.

I dialled the number that the porter gave me; I was lucky. Alec Palmer's voice answered; it was a pleasant-sounding voice. I told him about Carol.

I knew he was coming to Ambersea, this afternoon; and then everything happened at once. Louise was pouring the tea when the doorbell rang. Anyone who had known Louise would simply have walked in, so I guessed it wasn't a client. I hurried to answer the door. As I expected it was Alec who stood there, a tall, fair man with tired eyes, who looked past me, saw his wife half-turning to see who was at the door, and called her name.

'Carol!'

She started violently, rocking the step-ladder. Too late, I saw what was happening. Carol lost her balance, and crashed to the floor.

I raced over to her, one thought uppermost in my mind.

'Ring David!' I called urgently to Louise.

'Carol! Carol!' Alec was bending over the still, small figure. She looked small and lost and pathetic. Long before David and the ambulance arrived, I knew that Carol was going to lose the baby. This is my punishment for meddling, I thought aghast. I have done this.

I went to hospital with her in the ambulance. They let me see her for a few minutes that evening; she lay in a side ward, still and quiet, her red hair the only touch of colour, bright as a flame against the pillow. She gave me a twisted little smile.

'No baby!' she murmured. 'That's because I didn't want it. I've lost it, and it serves me right.' Tears filled her eyes. 'Funny,' she added, with bitter humour, 'now I've lost the baby I want it. That should make you laugh. Perfect punishment for all I've done, isn't it!'

'Nonsense!' I retorted. 'Carol, there's someone waiting outside to see you.'

'Alec,' she said resignedly. 'How did he find me?'

'Does that matter? He's very anxious to see you. Sister says she'll give him five minutes with you. Can I send him in?'

'Yes,' she said reluctantly. She turned her head away, her eyes full of tears.

I went outside, and beckoned to Alec to go in. There was a world of love and tenderness in his voice as he entered he side-ward.

'Darling!' I heard him say softly. 'You're coming home – for good! In time for Christmas. Sweetheart, don't cry!'

I saw his arms go around her as I closed the door. The tears would heal, I thought, as they always did, and Carol was ready to go home, she had finally stopped running away from life and herself…

It was some days before I saw Louise again. She came up to tea with me one afternoon.

'Carol will be out of hospital next week,' she said. 'She's going home with her husband. I saw her today, and she said she'd like to see you before she left Ambersea.' Louise sighed. 'Julie, I'm so glad things have turned out the way they have; but *I'm* to blame for Carol losing the baby. I should never have let her climb the ladder.'

'No,' I argued. 'It was *my* fault! I telephoned Alec.'

I told Louise the whole story. She looked thoughtful when I had finished; finally, she said:

'Let's say it was an ill wind, Julie; or something that was meant to be. Perhaps we're both blaming ourselves too much.

'It's the one guilty secret I shall keep from David!' I told her ruefully. 'I'm sure he wouldn't approve, even though Carol has her husband back again.'

I saw Carol just before she left Ambersea with Alec. She was sitting in Louise's sitting-room, a quiet little figure, much of her flamboyance gone. She seemed older, more subdued, and she looked at Alec as though she was afraid he was going to vanish; he had an air of protective tenderness towards her. I knew that everything was going to be all right for the Palmers. Not yet; not, perhaps for a long time. But Carol had been given a second chance, and I hoped she would take it. For these two, Christmas would be a new beginning.

'Thank you for all you have done for my wife,' Alec told us both.

'I'm sorry you had such a bad time with me!' Carol said, with something of her old flippant air; but her eyes asked for understanding.

As I was leaving, she came to the door.

'I really am grateful to you and Miss Whittaker,' she said awkwardly. 'Alec says you got in touch with him. I wanted him so much, and I *couldn't* – not when I was expecting Mark's baby!' Her face crumpled for a moment, then she added:

'He was so understanding. I asked him today if he would have felt the same about taking me back if I hadn't lost the baby, and he says it would have made no difference to him. He's wonderful. He *must* love me...!'

'That's true love,' I told her.

'I know.' Her eyes were brilliant with tears. 'I'll never be fooled again; I was just infatuated with Mark. I want another baby, Mrs Pembury – Alec's and mine.'

'Tell him so,' I said. 'It will be the best Christmas present you can give him.'

Louise and I watched them drive away; it was very cold and a few stray snowflakes began to drift lazily from the sky, giving a Christmas card touch to the quiet road. At the corner, Carol turned and waved to us.

'Well, come along!' Louise said briskly, blowing her nose. 'Time we got the rest of those decorations up!'

I went to help her, thinking about David, and my small, guilty secret. This would be our first married Christmas. I hoped that, for the Palmers, Christmas would be just as wonderful as it was going to be for David and me.

CHAPTER 4

January is a horrible month, I thought, looking at the rain beating with steady persistence against the surgery windows. It was a day for staying indoors, and I knew David would have a full surgery on such a morning.

Looking back at Christmas warmed my day, though; my first Christmas as Dr David Pembury's wife.

David poked his head around the door of the surgery and smiled at me.

'Everything ready for you, Doctor!' I told him.

'Thanks, Nurse!' He kissed me, as though he hadn't seen me for months, instead of less than an hour ago at breakfast!

'Full surgery?' he asked.

''Fraid so, darling! And a big round for you, afterwards, too! Not surprising – just *look* at the weather!'

It was almost midday before David set out on his rounds. The rain was still coming down fiercely, and I had just finished eating a solitary lunch when the telephone rang. It was Sally Allister.

'Hello, Julie!' she said. *'Isn't* this a wretched day!'

'Mm!' I agreed. 'You don't sound very happy, and I'm not sure the weather is to blame, somehow!' I told her.

Her laugh sounded wry.

'Julie, you have a sixth sense about other people's troubles!' She sighed. 'I think I'll come over and talk to you.'

'Lovely!' I told her. 'I've got a free afternoon and a new-baked cake. If you promise to leave a slice for David, you can come and share both, plus a pot of tea!'

I wondered what was wrong; not Sally's marriage – she was blissfully happy. Something at the store, I reflected…

Sally drove herself over in the little white car that had been her father's wedding present; coming motherhood suited her – she looked absurdly young and rather sweet in her big, brightly-coloured coat.

She looked gratefully at the blazing fire, and settled herself in the armchair, as I poured tea.

'It's time you gave up working at the store!' I told her bluntly.

'I *am* giving up – early next month!' She pulled a face at me. 'I'm thrilled about the baby, though I've enjoyed having something to do all this long time of waiting. Father will be able to manage – he's got a wonderful staff. I want to leave things nice and tidy, Julie; and I'm worried!' She spread her hands to the blaze, and added:

'Remember, a few months ago, I told you we'd taken on a new store detective – a Mrs Grace Lombard? You've seen her in the shop, Julie.'

I thought back; yes, I remembered. A well-built woman in her late forties, with smooth, pale hair cut severely short; a hard face, and very alert eyes behind glasses with heavy horn-rims.

'Don't you like her?' I guessed.

'As a person – no,' Sally conceded reluctantly. 'I've tried! But she's not easy to know; hard, very reserved – and over-zealous. Almost as though she has to keep on proving herself. And a store detective must be very careful, as you know. A false accusation can cause untold damage where the good name of a shop is concerned; last week, Stella Stevens was in the store; her mother is one of our best customers, and Stella goes to college next year. She came in and bought some cosmetics and stockings. I saw Mrs Lombard making a bee line towards her, with a purposeful look in her eye – Stella took a box of face powder out to the street, to see it in daylight. She's at an age where she's terribly fussy about cosmetics. Well, I just stopped Grace Lombard in time ... Stella didn't notice anything wrong, fortunately, and I asked Mrs Lombard to come along to my office, later.'

'What happened?' I asked.

'It must have been obvious to Grace Lombard that she had made a mistake. I checked with the girl on cosmetics, in front of Mrs Lombard, just to be absolutely certain.'

'And Mrs Lombard didn't like being proved wrong?' I said.

'She was sullen and resentful about it. *Think* what it would have meant, if she had accused Stella!' Sally shuddered. 'I pointed that out to her. I didn't make any impres-

83

sion. But that's not the worst, Julie. Last Saturday, young Sandra Allison came in with a crowd of teenagers.'

My heart went down like a stone through a pool of water.

'What happened?' I asked.

'Sandra and half a dozen other girls were milling around the costume jewellery counter. That counter is one of the best patronized by shop-lifters, I know, and Mrs Lombard pays it particular attention! Well, it seems that a ring was missed from its show stand and was found in Sandra's shopping basket.

'Grace Lombard brought Sandra to me; and Sandra insisted that one of the other girls with her had taken the ring, and dropped it in *her* basket. In fact,' Sally added wryly, 'she showed me how it was done! Very ingenious. Just pick up a velvet show-stand with rings in the slots, try one of them on, while your friends admire, and then decide you like another one on another stand much better! You forget to take off the first ring, and while you're holding up the second velvet stand, your fingers are busy at the back of the stand, slipping off the ring, dropping it into basket or bag! I must say Sandra gave a very neat demonstration! I believe she was telling the truth, Julie – oh, no, not because she was one of your protégés! Just a feeling I had. She was scared to death, but I'm sure she wasn't lying! I gave

84

her a pretty sharp talking-to about going around with a bunch of youngsters like that, and told her not to come into the store again!' Sally finished unhappily. 'Then I sent her home.'

'What did Mrs Lombard say?'

Sally spread her hands helplessly.

'She was furious, of course! Thoroughly unpleasant – said I was trying to make things impossible for her, that I had a grudge against her, and if I was gullible enough to believe Sandra Allison's story I wasn't capable of running a store! I almost lost my temper. I told her I thought she should leave Carmichael's, and she retorted that if she was dismissed, then she would sue for wrongful dismissal, and make things very unpleasant all round! Oh, *Julie!*' Sally's eyes were full of tears. 'She was horrible – so *spiteful!* I just don't understand! She's bitter and unhappy, and the *last* kind of person who should be a store detective, and I wish she'd just leave! I can understand her being mad with me, after I'd ticked her off about Stella – but this was pure hatred! I think she hates everyone!'

Poor Sally! She looked so forlorn that I put an arm around her shoulders. I knew what was worrying her. Carmichael's took great pride in the fact that they had a happy staff – and Sally must have found Grace Lombard's venom hard to understand; she didn't want to leave her father's store with *that* particular memory.

'What's bothering you most?' I asked slowly. 'Is it because you think Mrs Lombard may have been right, and Sandra did steal the ring?'

'No. Grace Lombard was so full of outraged virtue. She *wanted* Sandra to be guilty, somehow! She was so triumphant, so scornul because I let Sandra go home!'

'Don't waste any more tears on it,' I told her. 'You did what you believed to be right.'

Sally wasn't easily comforted; but when I sent her home, she was smiling, though rather wanly. I told David about it, over our evening meal.

'Poor Sally!' he said gently. 'She's overdoing it! A good thing she's leaving in a week or two – she may be fit and well, and having a perfectly normal pregnancy, but she's also over-sensitive and easily upset, at this stage.'

I knew David was right. I also knew Sally, gay and warm-hearted, was unused to dealing with people like Mrs Lombard.

Sally had insisted that Grace Lombard was suffering from more than an attack of over-vigilance where her job was concerned. I went into Carmichael's next morning, and saw Mrs Lombard; she was standing by the stocking counter.

Her cold eyes flicked over me, from head to toe. I could well imagine that she was a formidable enemy. She was precisely and faultlessly dressed. Her mouth was tight, she looked a woman without warmth or softness, and I wondered about her, as I went along to visit the Allisons.

Sandra Allison answered the door. She looked at me warily, and stood aside, with some reluctance, for me to come in to the big, untidy sitting-room, where the 'babies', Heather and Paul, were battling amiably over possession of a teddy-bear.

'Shirley's out,' Sandra said shortly. 'Gone to get the weekend shopping. She always does on Saturday afternoons. Lorraine went with her. Dad's at football.'

'How are *you*?' I asked brightly.

'All right.' She shrugged; she still looked at me warily, but I could tell that she was miserable.

I felt so sorry for her, halfway between childhood and being a young adult; a thin girl in a mini-skirt, a brilliantly-coloured sweater, and shoes with heels that were too high and somehow only emphasised her vulnerability. She had been trying out a new hair-style that didn't suit her, and she pushed at it, nervously, with one hand. It had been difficult enough for Shirley to take over the job of 'mothering' the family; equally difficult for Sandy, I thought compassionately, to grow up without a mother. Even a tolerant, good-natured elder sister

87

could never be anything but a sad substitute.

I didn't know what to say to her. David has told me so many times that I rush in where angels fear to tread, and he's right. I'm a born meddler, and it often lands me in trouble.

'You don't look very happy,' I said gently. 'Anything I can do?'

'Nothing.' She tried to sound airy; then, suddenly, her thin veneer of false sophistication cracked wide.

'Shirley's mad with me!' she said. 'She keeps on and *on* about it! And it wasn't my fault. A crowd of us went down to Carmichael's – some of the girls from school – and one of them pinched a ring, and I got the blame...'

The story tumbled out, indignantly told; and yet I, too, could have sworn she was telling the truth; and I made a mental note to have a tactful word with Shirley about delivering a lecture and leaving it at that, although I guessed that Shirley's nagging probably sprang from feeling worried and uneasy. Apparently Shirley had told Mr Allison, and Sandra had been in hot water with her father, too.

'This girl who took the ring – Jenny Johnson – has she ever taken anything before, that you know of?' I asked.

'Yes. She showed us how to do it, but we

were too scared. She said she gets *lots* of things that way and you don't get caught if you're smart!' Sandy said pertly.

'She's wrong; most people get caught in the end,' I retorted. 'She's very stupid not to realise that – and you're asking for trouble yourself, if you go around with girls like Jenny!'

'Oh, sure!' She shrugged again, with weary, almost adult resignation that lit the situation with faint humour for me, briefly. 'Dad said I wasn't to see her again. I didn't take the wretched ring, honest...'

'I believe you,' I told her. 'But your father's right. The next time it happens, you might come up in front of someone less understanding than Miss Carmichael; and then you'll *really* be in trouble. It isn't worth it...'

I had the consolation of seeing Sandy look a little happier when I left; she had probably learnt her lesson, I thought.

When I met Sally for lunch, a few days later, I told her about my meeting with Sandra. The fact that I believed Sandy was innocent seemed to comfort Sally, although she told me that Mrs Lombard was still being difficult and unpleasant.

'Never mind!' I consoled. 'Your father will know how to deal with her, when he takes over...!'

'That's just it, Julie! I feel, in some way,

89

that this is my fault, and I don't see why he should inherit my troubles! Grace Lombard loses no opportunity of insinuating that I don't know how to treat staff...'

Well, it wouldn't be Sally's worry much longer, I thought.

As it happened, it was almost a month before I saw Sally again. David was terribly busy, and I worried a great deal about him; he came home each night, exhausted, to face a surgery that didn't seem as if it could hold any more people.

And then suddenly the worst was over; the queue of patients at the surgery door, and on the other end of our telephone, thinned out, and we had a respite. We went out into the country one Saturday afternoon to discover dusty lambs'-tails catkins swinging from bare trees, and snowdrops clustered in cottage gardens; it was a mild day, with the merest suspicion of warmth in the pale sunshine, and we were blissfully happy.

'Kathy is coming to supper this evening,' I reminded David.

We both liked shy, gentle little Kathy Jessop, who had been my friend since I began district nursing in Ambersea, and later, my bridesmaid, when I married David. It would be fun to talk 'shop', I thought happily.

As it happened, David was unexpectedly called out that evening. He left us, soon after we had finished our evening meal, and Kathy and I dawdled over coffee, by the fire. Kathy brought me bits of gossip about old patients of mine, about the Nurses' Home. I reminded her of my first day as district nurse, when she had told me not to worry about Mrs Whittaker's sharp tongue.

'Oh, her bark was worse than her bite!' Kathy agreed. 'I wouldn't call her really difficult; the really tough cases are those like my latest – Mrs Lombard. There's a woman I can't get near; she's obviously unhappy and lonely, and it's not helping her...'

'Tell me about her,' I said.

'Well, she lives alone. She's a widow – her husband died only a few years after she was married, I believe. She had a daughter; pretty girl – I've seen a photo of her. Killed in a car accident. That's all I know. Grace Lombard lives by herself in her spotless little flat, and believes in keeping herself to herself. Result: she's put up a high fence that no one can climb over. And I can't help feeling that the fence needs to come down.'

'What has been wrong with her?'

'Acute appendicitis. She left hospital last week. I go in once a day; she says she can manage...' Kathy shrugged and smiled ruefully at me.

I telephoned Sally next morning.

'Hello, Julie!' she said gaily. 'I must say it's nice to be at home! Carmichael's dismissed me last week – didn't you know?'

It was good to hear Sally sounding so happy. She told me about the gifts with which she had been presented by the staff.

'How is Mrs Lombard?' I asked.

'She left – she was taken ill at work – acute appendicitis. I sent her flowers and good wishes, but she made it quite clear she didn't want either, and that she wasn't coming back to Carmichael's to work. I must be honest, Julie, and admit *that* was a relief. As you said once, problems have a way of solving themselves, sometimes.'

Yet I felt that Grace Lombard's problems were far from solved; I told David so.

'Now, Julie!' he warned, half serious, half teasing. 'If ever there was a clear case of "No Trespassers" it's Grace Lombard! You can't help some people because they don't want to be helped.'

'Who says I'm going to help her?' I murmured. 'I'm just going to take her some books!'

David cast his eyes up to heaven in mock dismay.

'Books – the classic excuse for a visit!' he said.

'But a good one!' I retorted stubbornly.

The best one, I thought; for people who are sick are often lonely as well, and too proud to admit it. Books open many doors, as once my uniform opened doors for me.

Now I had an 'understanding' with Miss Verney, the Superintendent of our District Nurses' Home, that I could be a kind of unofficial 'follow-up' visitor for patients who need cheering up as much as physical care.

Even Miss Verney, however, was dubious, when I telephoned next morning, though she readily agreed that I *might* be able to do something for Grace Lombard.

I found her flat without much difficulty – on the second floor of a modern block of flats near the seafront. She came to the door wearing a severely-cut housecoat. She was thinner, but her eyes and mouth looked as hard as ever.

'Yes?' she said uncompromisingly.

'I thought you might like some books,' I said. I added, casually, that I was a kind of 'mobile library' for Miss Verney. The explanation apparently satisfied her, but she admitted me to her flat with some reluctance.

It was just as I had expected it would be – spotless, perfect, every cushion neatly plumped, every ashtray and ornament placed at a precise angle. I couldn't imagine children playing here, or people gathered for a happy, friendly evening.

I looked pointedly at the tea-tray set with one cup and saucer.

'Would you like a cup of tea?' Grace Lombard asked stiffly.

'Love one!' I told her.

When she had gone to the kitchen, I picked up the only photograph in the room. It was silver-framed and stood alone on a small table.

I studied the face; a girl of about eighteen, pretty, with a warm smile and soft fair hair. Something about her was vaguely familiar. *Sandra!* I thought. *She* had the same thin face and loose fair hair. Sandra was younger, but, at eighteen, she would look very much like this girl...

Grace Lombard came back into the room as I was examining the photograph.

'What an attractive girl!' I said sincerely.

'My daughter.' Busy at the tea-tray, she did not look up. 'She died three years ago. Milk? Sugar, Mrs–?'

'Pembury,' I said quickly. Surely, I thought, puzzled, Grace Lombard could not be washed of all emotion as she would have me believe?

'Do you live on your own?' I enquired tentatively.

'Yes – my husband died before Anne was born.' Mrs Lombard studied me intently. 'I've seen you somewhere before, Mrs Pembury.'

'Shopping in Carmichael's, perhaps,' I said warily.

'Ah yes! I was their store detective until recently. There's far too much pilfering going on nowadays, especially among young people! They seem to think they can have what they want from life, without paying for it – or getting found out. I took great pride in my work, there...'

Her vehemence puzzled me. She made several other caustic remarks about present-day teenagers being shallow and selfish; if I had tried to reason with her, she would have swept my words away like autumn leaves on a great gale of angry words. So I merely asked her if she planned to return to Carmichael's.

'No,' she said shortly. 'I didn't see eye to eye with my employer. She made my work quite impossible by being much too lenient with the culprits! They should be punished, more strictly supervised!'

Grace, who had showed no feeling for her daughter, showed so much bitterness for the youngsters of her daughter's age. I was puzzled.

I made no progress with Grace Lombard. No, she had no idea what she intended to do when she was well enough to work; no, she was never lonely, and thank you, it was kind of me to call, but now she had several things that needed her attention...

I went home feeling thoroughly deflated. David's sympathy had a faintly 'I-told-you-so' flavour.

I rang Sally the following morning.

'Tell me,' I said thoughtfully, 'what does Stella Stevens look like? You know, the girl Grace Lombard almost picked up, in error...?'

'Yes, of course I remember. Stella? Well, she's small and fair and quiet; a nice girl. Why, Julie?'

'Just a theory I have,' I told her.

I took snowdrops and some more books to Mrs Lombard, some days later. She admitted me to the flat with the same reluctance that she had shown the first time, and showed no pleasure in the flowers; but she offered me a cup of tea, as though she felt she owed it to me.

I drank it, making conversation and feeling, dismally, that I had failed with Mrs Lombard; whatever went on behind that smooth, quiet face, she was as tightly-closed as an oyster to anything approaching friendliness. But when I mentioned her work, once again there was an angry tirade against teenagers.

I was just finishing my second cup of tea when I happened to casually mention Sandra Allison. I hadn't meant to do so, but we were talking about embroidery, and I happened to mention that Sandra was a wonderful needlewoman.

The thin eyebrows went up sharply.

'Do you know her well?' Grace Lombard asked.

All right, Julie! I thought grimly. No sense in beating about the bush!

'Pretty well; I know the whole family, in fact. I like them...'

'Sandra Allison is a very accomplished little thief!' Grace said coldly.

I couldn't let that pass.

'But you're wrong! She told me about it – and so did Sally...'

And then it came out, in a furious spate of words – fury, resentment, bitterness that had been held back too long.

'So you're a friend of Mrs Allister's too? No doubt you hold the same views that teenagers should be mollycoddled? She doesn't need a store detective; I told her so! She should just let them help themselves, as they please!'

'Mrs Lombard,' I said, as calmly as I could, 'why are you so bitter against youngsters, in particular? You had a daughter of your own!'

'Oh yes!' she retorted. 'Born a month after her father died! It wasn't easy to bring up a daughter properly, and educate her well. It meant doing without luxuries; it meant hard work – and loneliness, as well. I thought Anne was worth it. She grew up to be a pretty girl, Mrs Pembury; she was eighteen, and had a place at University – I was so *proud* of her, so thrilled; all the years of going without, of managing and making do, had been worthwhile. And then do you know what happened? She got in with a wild crowd. Parties and dances and having a good time – that's all they ever thought about! They helped themselves to what they couldn't afford to buy – they weren't content to wait and work and save. Anne was convicted of shoplifting: she took a brooch from one of the big stores. She told me she had done it for a dare; and she was put on probation. I couldn't *believe* that *my* daughter had done such a dreadful thing.'

I heard the agony in her voice, under the fury. I felt compassion for them both – the girl brought up within narrow limits, dazzled, tempted, urged on by people who had probably seemed to be gay and sophisticated; a moment's folly, the knowledge that her mother would never understand. And Grace, bewildered, not knowing where she had gone wrong; perhaps, I thought, she had been too strict with Anne.

'I'm sorry!' I said inadequately.

'Sorry?' Grace's laughter was hard and unamused. 'That's what Anne said. I told her I would never forgive her!'

'We've all done things for which we need forgiveness,' I pointed out.

'I don't need a sermon, Mrs Pembury!' Grace looked fleetingly at the photograph. 'I made great sacrifices for Anne, for her future – and *look* what happened! She was out with her boy-friend, in his father's car. I never liked him; he was the worst of them all, wild and silly, and a show-off! She knew I disliked him. He drove the car into a tree, and he and Anne were killed outright. Perhaps that was the best thing, after all the disgrace she had brought on us both!'

I was so horrified by her last remark, that tact and sympathy flew out of the window. I lost my temper. '"The best thing"?' I cried. 'That's terribly unfair – *and* I think you know it! By what you say, things weren't easy for *Anne,* either, when she was growing up. She had to work and study hard, to get her University place; there weren't many luxuries in *her* life. She was young – a bit wild, a bit careless, maybe – breaking out of a tight little shell, meeting people who probably seemed out of this world to her, different and dazzling. She lost her sense of proportion! She took a brooch for a dare – how pathetic that sounds! She needed your understanding, and you had none to give! And so you decide to go on punishing not only Anne, but anyone like her! Sandy reminded you of Anne – so did Stella! All you're doing is building up a great store of bitterness. Is *that* what you want? Is *that* how little your daughter meant to you?'

Grace's face was bright pink, her eyes like ice.

'I don't need your advice on how to run

my life, nor your opinions as to how I should have treated my daughter!' she retorted.

'But it's true; to go on punishing someone you love, through other people, is so senseless, so wrong...'

'I'd be glad if you'd leave!' Grace replied. 'I don't want any more magazines, thank you! I don't need anything from anyone!'

'Yes, you do!' I retorted, as I left the flat. 'Only maybe you'll realise that when it's too late!'

She shut the door sharply and finally behind me. By the time I reached home, I had cooled down a good deal. I told David about it, and he ruffled my hair understandingly.

'Never mind, darling! You tried; you can't do more. You'll have to write Mrs Lombard off as one of your failures!'

I knew he was right, but I hated having to do that, especially when, deep down, I felt tremendous pity for her.

I told Sally about it; she agreed with David that there was nothing anyone could do. Grace Lombard had the fixed idea that every teenager was a potential criminal who had to be caught and punished ... especially anyone who reminded her of Anne...

I tried to forget about it; I almost did until a few days later when I met Louise Whittaker.

She told me that her latest venture was helping at the Youth Club in the evenings.

'Julie,' she said, 'you meet plenty of people. If you – or Miss Verney – know of some lonely soul who would like something to do in the evenings, there's a job waiting for them at the Club. Pouring teas and coffees and keeping our little canteen going. I'm so busy myself with the games, and drama side, and we've no one...'

'I *might* be able to help,' I promised.

David says I never know when I'm defeated. I didn't dare to tell him that I was going to approach Grace Lombard.

I almost wished I hadn't decided to approach her, when I stood outside her flat, my finger against the bell.

She didn't even ask me in; she stood there, cold-eyed, and condemning as she looked me over.

'Well?' she said shortly.

Haltingly, I explained about the canteen; I made it sound as attractive as I could. I knew I had lost when I saw the thin, contemptuous smile on her mouth.

'I imagine you think it will be good for me, Mrs Pembury? A kind of therapy – get her out among young people and she'll see that they are all charming and innocent and delightful! And she'll forget that her daughter was a thief – like the Allison child–!'

I cut across her words.

'I don't think anything of the kind! I simply felt it might help you, take you out of yourself, to be with people. You're a lonely, bitter woman, Mrs Lombard, and determined to stay that way. You forget that people are frail and human and full of faults; that people don't always steal from complicated motives, but just because they see something pretty and want it; it's that simple. Or maybe they're with an irresponsible crowd, and they're frightened to be thought not one of the crowd. *You've* apparently never done anything wrong in your life, so how can you understand your fellow human beings?' I told her.

'I don't know why you go to so much trouble!' Grace retorted.

'I believe people are worth it; I always shall, in spite of your trying to convince me that they aren't!' I told her.

I went home – wept, and made myself a large pot of tea, thankful that David was out. I confided in Sally, who was sympathetic, and told me gently I was just wasting my time.

I thought so, too; and then, a week later, I met Kathy Jessop, going into a café for her mid-morning coffee.

I joined her, and we chatted together about patients.

'I'm glad I've seen you,' Kathy told me. 'I

102

visited Mrs Lombard for the last time a couple of days ago and she gave me a message; said if I saw you, I was to ask you to call at the flat...'

My heart lifted; it took wings and soared; but as I went to Grace Lombard's flat, I told myself not to expect miracles. They just don't happen; people don't change, suddenly – district nursing had taught me that much.

I rang the bell nervously, wondering what Grace Lombard could possibly have to say to me.

She looked the same – well, not quite. Her mouth wasn't so tight, I told myself, nor her eyes so cold; her 'Come in, Mrs Pembury' was quite impersonal.

'Sit down,' she said.

She poured tea. As I lifted my cup, I saw her watching me, thoughtfully, as though she was seeing me for the first time.

'No,' she said, as though in answer to my unspoken question, 'I haven't changed my mind; I don't intend to help at the Youth Club.'

I realised she wasn't ready for that particular challenge. I saw my mistake in trying to push her into a situation with which she could not yet cope; but, as I opened my mouth to apologise, she went on talking.

'I owe you an apology, Mrs Pembury. I have regretted speaking to you as I did. It was wrong of me; you were trying to help.'

'Most inadequately, I'm afraid,' I answered ruefully.

'No,' she admitted. 'You made me think. Thinking is a painful business,' she added with difficult, grudging honesty. 'Perhaps I *am* wrong in blaming Anne so bitterly. Perhaps her life was too austere. You can't answer those questions for me – only I can answer them.'

Some of her bitterness against her lost daughter had already gone, I thought happily. That was a small miracle, one I held gently and thankfully, not quite believing it had happened.

'Anyway,' she added crisply, 'the future can take care of itself as regards a job. I don't know what I shall do. For the present, I've drawn my savings and decided to take a three-week cruise in the Mediterranean. It's years since I had a decent holiday.'

I searched carefully for the right words. Not *'It will do you good, because you have lived too frugally, for too long.'* Something easy and casual.

'Lovely!' I told her. 'David and I have promised ourselves a year-long cruise when he retires. I doubt that we'll ever make it; something to dream of, though – a lovely, lazy holiday. I hope you enjoy it, Mrs Lombard!'

I stood up quickly. The look on her face

made me want to cry – I realised for the first time just how lonely she was.

'I'll send you a card,' she said, with a half-smile.

'I'd like that! The biggest, most glossy one you can find, remember!'

She put her hand on my arm, and I guessed that it was the first time she had touched another human being, spontaneously, for many a long day. She looked as though she was going to say something, changed her mind, and closed the door quickly – but not before I had seen that her eyes were too bright.

Idiot, I told myself, walking home! What are *you* crying for? *You* haven't anything to cry about!

Ah, but there are tears and tears! And David, who understands me better than I do myself, put it in a nut-shell, when I reached home.

He came out of the surgery, closed the door, and looked at me thoughtfully.

'You've been crying, Julie,' he said. 'Your nose is pink and you look as though someone had just given you the fairy from the top of the Christmas tree. Which means that something has unexpectedly turned out right for you, just when you least expected it.'

He came over and kissed me.

'Let's make some tea,' he suggested. 'And

you can tell me all about it!'

Dear David! I'm so lucky, I thought. I hope that, one day, Grace Lombard will again find the special kind of happiness that comes from loving and being loved.

CHAPTER 5

I knew it was spring, as soon as I awoke that morning; there was a blackbird singing in the garden, and, propping myself up on one elbow, I could see the big tree covered with tiny green buds. The sky was blue – really blue, not the washed-out colour that passes for blue in February.

This was March. Tomorrow, I thought, will be our wedding anniversary – I shall have been married to David for a year; it doesn't seem possible.

I looked at his sleeping face, the ruffled dark hair making him look young and vulnerable. I dropped a kiss lightly on his cheek and he stirred and sighed.

I had been a brand-new district nurse when we had first met; I still remembered, with amusement, that we had quarrelled fiercely at our first meeting, and disliked one another for a long time afterwards; but now – almost a year married, and no quarrels, I thought smugly.

I said as much to David, at breakfast.

'Mm.' He put down his coffee-cup, his eyes amused. 'A year married, and we still, apparently, are in the running for the Dunmow Flitch? My love, if that's a gentle way of reminding me that tomorrow is our anniversary, it's not necessary!' He looked pleased with himself. 'I ringed it on the surgery calendar. No surgery tomorrow night; dinner for two at the Bay Hotel where I proposed to you. I might even buy you a present to mark the occasion, if you're good!'

I made a face at him. David in this mood gave me a glimpse of the boy he had once been. If ever we have a son, I reflected, I hope he will be just like David.

I had bought David some rather special cuff-links for the occasion. I wanted an anniversary card, and I also had some other bits and pieces of shopping to do. In Carmichael's store, I dawdled at the fabrics counter, and finally bought a length of material in a heavenly blue shade that was a mad extravagance. Well, most women go overboard for hats in the spring, I thought – and I don't wear hats! Besides, little Miss Laura McCade, dressmaker, who had once been a patient of mine, would make it up beautifully and inexpensively.

I had lunch at the Nurses' Home with

Miss Verney. What memories it brought back for me – and what a joy it was to talk 'shop' with this deceptively-fragile-looking little woman who looked after 'her nurses' so wonderfully well and who always told me when she had patients needing visitors, so that I would not feel completely out of touch with my old life. Being David's surgery nurse was wonderful, but my old patients were my friends and I still liked to see them.

I walked home by way of the sea-front; and there I met Shirley Allison, out with her young brother Paul.

'Hello, Nurse Barden!' she said. 'Oh, I keep forgetting, it's Mrs Pembury – Sandra is always ticking me off about that! I'm glad I've seen you; I've got some *wonderful* news. I've had a letter from Mum! She's going to come and see us!'

To say I was astounded puts it much too mildly. It was more than two years since Mrs Allison had left her husband and five children to go away with another man. Shirley had been sixteen, then, and had looked after her four younger brothers and sisters with astonishing capability.

Now Shirley was eighteen, engaged to Joe Soames. Sandra was fifteen, and soon she would be taking over Shirley's job of looking after nine-year-old Lorraine, Heather who was starting school in the autumn – and four-year-old Paul.

I looked at Shirley – bright-eyed, her red hair blowing in the breeze, excitement in her face.

'So you're pleased?' I said cautiously.

'Of course I am! Look, here's the letter!' She dived into her handbag and thrust it at me. 'You can read it!'

There was an address and a telephone number elaborately printed on the sheet of notepaper. Marlingham: it was a big busy town. Mrs Allison's letter covered only one side of the paper and said simply that she thought she would like to see her family again, and would come to Ambersea for the day – she would let them know when...

I hid my amazement. A woman who had left her husband and family without a word for more than two years, to live with another man, calmly suggesting she might call on them again!

'What does your father think about it?' I asked, handing back the letter.

'Oh!' Shirley pulled a face, watching Paul skim stones into the water. 'He doesn't like the idea at all! Says he doesn't want to see her. He said he supposed he couldn't stop her from seeing *us* if she wanted to, but *he* isn't going to be there. Men!' she said, so wrathfully that I half-smiled. 'Well, *I'll* be pleased to see mum, anyway. Gosh, wait till she sees how Sandy has grown, and when I tell her I'm engaged...!'

'What about your mother's man-friend – the one she's living with?' I asked bluntly.

Shirley coloured, and then said defensively:

'Do you know what *I* think? I think it's all over, and she wishes she'd never gone away and wants to come back to us all. I told Dad so. Anyone can make a mistake – or do something wrong and silly and then be sorry afterwards!'

Oh, Shirley, I thought, you're so young to be such a philosopher about some of life's biggest issues!

'Anyway,' Shirley added, 'she'll get a big welcome from me, never mind what Dad feels like. Oh, I suppose he felt pretty sore at what she did. I think the trouble was, there were too many of us. *Five!* It got her down, you know – she used to say she couldn't cope – but now we're older, it will be different.'

'I hope so,' I said gently. 'I'm so pleased your mother is coming back; and I hope it's for good.'

'I'm going to write to her tonight!' Shirley promised, 'and tell her to come home as soon as she likes.'

I couldn't wait to tell David the news, that evening.

'Isn't it good news?' I said, as we sat talking over a pot of tea, when his last patient

110

had left the surgery. 'I'm so glad Mrs Allison has come to her senses at last – and it must have been very difficult for Shirley, coping all on her own. However hard she tries, she can never take her mother's place.'

'Perhaps not,' David retorted, 'but if you or Shirley think any problems will be solved by Mrs Allison coming home, you're wrong. Her return will only produce a fresh crop of problems!'

'But, David!' I said, aghast, 'it's the best thing for them all! I thought you would have seen that!'

'Best thing for whom? For Mr Allison, who has made it quite clear that he cannot forgive or forget?'

'You're so Victorian!' I cried impatiently. 'In time, he'll forgive…'

'Maybe. I doubt it, very much. And he'll never forget; the first time they disagree, it will become the pivot on which their quarrel revolves. She'll be resentful, and she won't find it any easier to cope with five youngsters simply because they are two years older than when she went away. She'll hate being tied down – it seems her gentleman-friend has money, to provide her with headed notepaper and a telephone. Her husband doesn't earn all that much; if she could abandon her family once, she can do it again – but not before she and her husband have quarrelled so often and so bitterly that it's going to reflect on the children. They've learnt to do without her. Much better that she should stay where she is, and leave Shirley to get on with a job she's doing very well!'

'But what about Shirley?' I retorted. 'She wants to get married; even if Sandy takes over the care of the three youngsters, the children *need* their mother!'

'They've done pretty well without her for a long time now!' David argued stubbornly. 'You're a sentimental idiot, Julie – you're not seeing things in their proper perspective at all!'

And there we were – in the middle of our first real row, shouting at one another; until suddenly, I stopped and said, horrified:

'Oh, *David!* After what I said this morning – that we'd been married a year and never quarrelled! *Now* look at us!'

David came over and held me close, as I burst into tears.

'Not a quarrel,' he soothed. 'Just a disagreement – you and I are looking at the Allison family through different ends of the telescope!'

That was one of the nicest things about David – something I was discovering for the first time: that he would always come more than halfway to meet me when we disagreed.

'I'm an idiot! I said wryly. 'Why do I worry

about them, anyway?'

'Because you're made that way – and I love you for it,' he retorted. 'You know, you haven't flown at me in such a fury since the first day we met. I'd forgotten how sweet you look when you're angry.'

I laughed shakily, and clung to him, loving him with a fierce tenderness I could never put into words. Time, I thought, would show that I was right – and that Mrs Allison's homecoming would be the best thing for them all.

Neither David nor I mentioned the Allisons, by mutual agreement next day! There was a bouquet of spring flowers for me, delivered from the Flower Basket in the High Street, and David presented me with a piece of Victorian jewellery that had belonged to his mother. In the evening we went to the Bay Hotel and laughed happily together over the time David had tried to propose to me – and all the lights in the dining-room had fused, right in the middle of his proposal!

David toasted me in champagne.

'To our golden wedding,' he said, 'and hordes of grandchildren!'

'Oh, David,' I whispered, 'that's the one thing I need to make life complete! Children – you have to have *those* if you're to have grandchildren, you know!'

He patted my hand gently.

'Plenty of time, darling!' he reassured me.

Next day I took my length of material to Laura McCade, the dressmaker, who lived alone in a spotless little house near the seafront. She was always cheerful, brisk and busy and could perform miracles with a needle and a pair of scissors. Miss McCade had made my wedding dress, so I had a special affection for her.

However, I was surprised to find her less cheerful than usual. She looked strained and tired and put her hand to her head.

'Perhaps you've been doing too much sewing by artificial light,' I told her, remembering the long winter behind us.

'Maybe,' she agreed. 'My eyes have been bothering me a good deal lately. It's time I had my glasses changed – these are no use at all!'

She blinked at me, as though she couldn't see me clearly; I was worried. My professional training as a nurse had given me sharp eyes for many things, and I didn't like the look of Laura McCade. It wasn't just that she seemed under the weather; it was her eyes that bothered me.

I was reluctant to leave the material, telling her that it could be made up for me some other time when she was feeling better, but she was most indignant, and wouldn't hear of that.

'Well,' I said, 'be sure you get some new

glasses as soon as you can.'

'I'll ring Mr Simonds and make an appointment with him, first thing in the morning,' she promised.

I mentioned my worry to David that evening.

'If Mr Simonds finds anything really wrong he'll send her along to the Eye Hospital right away,' he reassured me.

I did not see Laura again for a week. I worried about her, and tried hard to clamp down on the suspicion that was beginning to form in my mind. I hoped I was wrong...

I met Shirley Allison on the day that I was due to go to Laura for a fitting. I saw her bobbing along happily, in her high heels, her bright hair flying like a banner, as she carried a loaded shopping basket.

I slowed down and opened the door.

'Jump in!' I said. 'I'll give you a lift home.'

'Thanks!' She was happy, and at the same time, ill at ease; soon enough, I knew, it would come tumbling out.

She invited me in for a cup of coffee. The house looked bright and tidy, and there were daffodils in the window. Shirley told me that Mrs Leigh, who cleaned David's surgery and 'baby-sat' sometimes for Shirley, had taken the two youngest children out for the day.

'Gives me time to catch up!' Shirley said. 'I want to wash the curtains and we need some new cushion covers in here...'

I smiled.

'You've heard from your mother again?' I guessed.

Shirley nodded.

'Yes; this morning. She's coming two weeks today. She doesn't say anything about coming home for good, but I'm sure she'll want to, as soon as she's inside the front door!' She sighed. 'If only Dad would be nicer about it. He's going to spoil things, Nurse Barden. He says he'll be here, after all, when Mum comes – to ask her just what she's going to do and tell her he doesn't want her back. Maybe she won't listen to him, if she knows how much *we* want her!'

Poor Shirley! She was on edge, tensed, fearing a scene that would spoil what was to be a wonderful homecoming.

'I'm sure your father will feel differently once your mother is back,' I told her. 'Don't worry, Shirley; everything will be all right, when your mother is here.'

Shirley looked unconvinced, and I felt annoyed with Mr Allison. Even if he did not feel he could forgive his wife, didn't he realise how much the children missed their mother? I could not believe, as David did, that the Allison children had learnt to do without their mother.

When I visited Laura McCade, I found her still looking tired and drawn; she told me that Mr Simonds had made an appointment for her to attend the local Eye Hospital, and I did not let her see how uneasy I felt. She fitted my dress with none of her usual briskness; she was slow and unsure of herself.

'Oh, I'm just tired!' she said, as though impatient with herself. 'I need a change. I'm going away to stay with an old friend of mine at Easter – it will do me good!'

She told me that the suit would be ready in two weeks' time.

I well remember the day I went to collect my suit; on that day Mrs Allison was due to come home. And it turned out to be a day when spring had deserted us; the skies were grey, the wind was sharp; the air smelt of rain, and the seas were tossing white foam angrily along the shingle.

I thought a great deal about Shirley that day; I hoped everything would go well for them all, and that John Allison would find some welcome in his heart for the wife who had left him.

Laura was a long time answering my knock. I knew at once that something was very wrong. She looked as grey as the day, listless and unhappy; she had been crying.

'What on earth is wrong?' I asked; but I *knew!* The fear that I had refused to acknowledge would no longer be pushed out of sight.

Without a word, Laura took me into the sitting-room. She sat down, not looking at me, and took off her glasses, turning them over and over in her hands as though any kind of action was better that just sitting still.

'I went to the Eye Hospital the day before yesterday,' she said. 'The specialist told me what was wrong with my eyes. He used a lot of long medical words, and then he explained what they meant: I can go on doing fine sewing, and reading and watching plenty of television – and lose my sight altogether. Or, he said, I can find a job that doesn't ask too much of my eyes, not read much or watch television very often – and with a good pair of glasses and using eye-drops every day, I'll probably keep a fair amount of sight.'

'Well,' I said, as cheerfully as I could, 'at least you know the worst – and what you can do about it.'

'Oh yes, I know *that!*' Her voice was bitter. 'What *shall* I do, Mrs Pembury? Go out and do other people's housework for them? Dressmaking is all I know how to do. I enjoy it; I'm making a success of my business. And now – *this!*'

I didn't know what to say to her; I sought desperately for some comfort to give. I thought of Sally Allister, and suggested that Sally might find a job at the store for her;

118

but Laura repudiated the suggestion indignantly, and with prickly pride.

'No, thank you. I'll think of something myself. Heaven knows what!' she said, still with that terrible bitterness in her voice. 'Life's so unfair! Just now, when I've been congratulating myself that things are going well. I might have known!'

'You feel bitter now,' I said gently, 'but it won't always seem so bad. You know that you won't lose your sight if you do as the specialist says; we must think of something else, something that you'd like to do. There's this house, for instance; all those rooms you don't use, and Louise Whittaker telling me only the other day that she was "house full" and did I know someone who would take in a couple of student teachers from the training college?'

'I don't want strangers in my house, thank you!' Laura McCade said, with pathetic dignity. 'I know you're trying to help, Mrs Pembury, but I shouldn't like other people around me.'

'You won't have them around you; they need a comfortable, quiet place in which to live when they aren't at college, and study. It wouldn't be such a bad thing to have someone else in the house.' I urged. 'You wouldn't feel so alone.'

She shrugged, as though she was too indifferent even to protest. I wanted so much to help and there was nothing I could say or do. I realised, too, that Laura's greatest need was going to be to find an outlet for her busy, active hands and brain; students might take care of some of her financial problems, but that wouldn't be enough.

'I'll come and see you again soon,' I promised; I'd ask Louise about it, I thought – she was a sensible, matter-of-fact person. I'd ask Sally, if there was anything she could do without Laura finding out; somehow, between us all, we could all help.

Of course, David was the first person to whom I told Laura's story.

'There isn't any easy solution, my love,' he told me gently. 'Whatever we can do for Laura – and there *are* things we can do to make it easier for her – the biggest hurdle is one we can't help her over: learning to adapt, to give up the one thing she has enjoyed doing, and made a success of; it's the kind of battle she will have to fight alone. All we can do is to be there, for she's going to need her friends.'

I sighed.

'Why is it there's never any straight-forward solution to life's toughest problems?' I asked him.

David looked rueful.

'Come to think of it,' he said, 'I'm not sure there's an easy solution to *any* of life's problems!'

I had forgotten about Mrs Allison's arrival, in my concern over Laura; but when I remembered, the next day, curiosity got the better of me – as David had predicted it would! I had potted some cuttings from one of my plants, and had promised it to Shirley – now seemed an ideal time to take it to her. I was longing to see Mrs Allison.

Shirley answered my knock.

'Hello,' she said flatly. 'Come in, Nurse.'

'Something wrong?' I asked.

'Oh – no, not really. Mum couldn't come. She's got 'flu. I only had the letter yesterday morning, and everything was ready. I made a cake – come in and try a piece!' Shirley managed a smile, and said with the optimistic elasticity of youth:

'Anyway, she'll come when she's better. She said so, in her letter. Dad's still against it, of course – and Sandy is siding with him!' Shirley said disgustedly.

'Don't worry,' I said gently, and with more optimism than I felt. 'I'm sure everything will be all right when your mother comes home.'

Louise Whittaker came to supper with us that evening. Both David and I were fond of brisk, energetic Louise who did so much good so quietly that it often passed unnoticed.

'I went to see Miss McCade after you phoned today,' she told me.

'Oh, Louise, I'm so glad! How was she?'

'Very unhappy. That's to be expected,' Louise said briskly. 'But she has agreed to take in a couple of students; I feel that it's a step in the right direction.'

I sighed, and said:

'She's still going to need something more – something to *do*...'

David looked from one to the other of us, a wicked twinkle in his eyes.

'Sitting here,' he said, 'I could almost be listening to two probation officers discussing their day's work!'

We laughed, and Louise retorted:

'You know perfectly well you wouldn't have it any other way!'

David winked at me – and gave me a look that seemed to sum up all the love and happiness we had known since our marriage.

I thought about Laura often, during the next few days; I thought about the Allisons, too. David managed to get a long weekend away and we went to visit my parents in Somerset. The weather was beautiful, and we picnicked out of doors, coming back to Ambersea refreshed and ready, as David said, for the longest queues outside the surgery doors!

So nearly three weeks passed. I visited Sally Allister, and taking a short cut home took me past the Allison house. Sandra was just going in, when I tooted my horn and stopped the car.

I wound down the window, and she came over to me; I saw that she was carrying a sheaf of iris and tulips. I guessed that they had been quite an expensive item in Sandy's budget.

'Hello!' she said; I thought she looked faintly disgruntled. She saw me glance at the flowers, and added:

'Mum's coming tomorrow. Shirley's had the house upside down for days. The *fuss!* Dad asked her last night if she was thinking of hiring a red carpet.' She pulled a face. 'They had quite a set-to about it! He's fed-up, and no wonder! Mum hasn't worried much about *us* the last couple of years, has she?'

'By which I gather that *you* aren't very pleased, either, at the thought of seeing your mother again?' I said.

Sandra considered, thoughtfully.

'Well, we're doing all right as we are,' she said finally. 'Anyway, what about this man she's living with? Is *he* going to let her come home just like that? I bet she'll be hankering to go back, after a bit, and then it'll be worse than ever, and the kids will be unsettled...'

I was startled. Sandra's voice and words held unexpected maturity that made her seem older than Shirley. I couldn't agree with her viewpoint – I was as sure as Shirley that Mrs Allison had finally faced up to her responsibilities as a mother – but certainly Sandra surprised me.

'Well,' I said lamely, 'I hope all goes well!'

All next day, Shirley and Laura remained tangled in my thoughts. I went to see Laura in the morning, and managed to persuade her to come and have coffee with me in a little sea-front café. She made an effort, but it wasn't easy for her; and I had learnt that one cannot force the pace of these things. As David had said, learning to adapt was the hurdle she had to take all alone.

I couldn't help feeling worried about Shirley. I was beginning to have the uneasy feeling that David had been right and that Mrs Allison's return could raise a fresh crop of problems.

Next day I called on the Allisons. I didn't even make a pretence of bringing books – I just wanted to know if everything had gone as Shirley had hoped it would.

I knocked twice. I thought there was no one at home – and then just as I was turning away, the door was opened.

Shirley stood there; she looked weary and dishevelled and her eyes were as red-rimmed as though she had been crying all night.

'*Shirley!*' I said, aghast. 'What's wrong?'

Listlessly, she held open the door.

'Come in,' she said.

The little sitting-room was unnaturally

tidy, full of flowers. She told me that Sandra had taken Paul and Heather to the park.

'Did your mother come yesterday?' I asked.

'No!' She sat down abruptly in the chair opposite me, letting the tears fall – angry, hurt, bewildered. I waited patiently.

'No, she didn't come! And she isn't going to, either! I got tea ready, and we waited and waited, and then I went to the telephone box. And do you know what Mum said, Nurse? That her *friend* didn't think she should come, after all!'

She put all the scorn in the world into that one word 'friend'.

'She could have let us know!' Shirley added miserably. 'Instead of just letting us wait and wait! I asked her if she was coming back for good, and she got quite mad with me, and said no, she never meant to, just to come for a visit. It was too much for her to manage, looking after the house and kids, she said. What about *me*?' Shirley put her hands to her eyes, as though to stop the flood of tears.

'She said she was very happy where she was; that she'd just suddenly felt she'd like to see us, that was all. And then she said she was going to ask Dad about a divorce ... oh, *he* doesn't care! He says it's the best thing!'

Shirley looked up at me, stricken. I felt totally inadequate. I went over and put my arms tightly around her, holding her close as though she was younger than Sandy. I had never hated anyone so much as I hated Mrs Allison at that moment.

I didn't say anything at all, until her tears stopped; even then, I wasn't sure that there was anything I could say that would ease the hurt, the disillusion. Shirley's world had crumbled – how could I possibly hope to put it together again, with a handful of words?

'Listen, Shirley,' I said gently. 'It's really better this way, although you don't think so now. If your mother *had* come back, your father would never have forgiven or forgotten what she had done, and that would have caused trouble between them. She wouldn't have found it any easier to look after you all than she did when she went away – and so she might go away again. That would be worse. The children would suffer; much better for your mother to stay where she is, and let you get on with the job you've been doing so well!'

Someone had said those words to *me,* not long ago. *David,* I thought, with wry amusement. For the first time I acknowledged that he had been right; so had Sandy. Shirley and I had been the sentimental ones, forgetting the practical issues.

'Oh, I suppose you're right!' Shirley said miserably. 'But I never thought *my* mum would turn out like this – run off with someone else and forget about her kids for a couple of years, and then want a divorce just because she found someone who could give her a good time. People are rotten! *I* don't want to get married!'

Ah, I thought – the disillusionment is hardest of all for Shirley to bear; particularly hard because it's her mother...

'Rubbish!' I said briskly. 'You're going to marry Joe and be happy. People aren't perfect, Shirley – they're very frail sometimes, especially where their feelings are involved. One day you may feel tempted, as your mother was – oh, you can shake your head, but it's quite easy to be tempted by prospects of freedom and more money. Don't expect too much of anyone, learn to accept them as they are, with their faults as well as their nice qualities. No one is all saint – or all sinner. Try to understand what made your mother behave as she did and tell yourself you aren't going to make the same mistakes. Now, that's the end of my lecture!' I added briskly. 'Do you feel like making me a cup of tea?'

She managed a tremulous half-smile that made me want to cry, for she looked so young, so vulnerable. She pushed away the last of the tears from her cheeks, squared her shoulders and said in an almost-normal voice:

'You can try some of the cake I made

yesterday; it's quite good.' Awkwardly, she put a hand on my arm as she went towards the kitchen.

'Thanks, Nurse!' she said.

It was, I thought, the nicest tribute I had ever received: Shirley's thanks, and the smile, uncertain though it was, that said she was learning to accept life with all its shades of black and white and grey.

I praised her flower arrangements, the new cushion covers she had made; told her she had every reason to be proud of the job she had done. And when I went home, she seemed, if not happier, to have some of her old bounce, her happy-go-lucky attitude towards life. Shirley, I reflected thankfully, would mend quickly.

I waited until evening surgery was over before I told David. It was our favourite time of day, a tranquil hour that belonged only to the two of us.

I carried a cup of tea across to him, as he sat in the armchair, listening to the last bird-songs.

'David,' I said, 'I owe you an outsize apology. You were entirely right about Mrs Allison, and I was all wrong. I didn't know just how wrong until I used your arguments to help Shirley today!'

I sat beside him, and told him the whole story. His arm went round my shoulders, then he lifted his hand and ruffled the back

128

of my hair in a familiar gesture.

'Apology accepted!' he told me gravely. Then he hugged me briefly.

'Sweetheart, I love you because you believe in what you do – not because you're always right. There's an important difference, you know! And now I have some news for you, Mrs Pembury. You haven't even noticed the bunch of flowers awaiting your kind attention in the kitchen!'

'Oh yes, I have!' I retorted. 'I wondered why? What have you broken, or is there some anniversary *I've* forgotten?'

'Neither! I've just been doing some of your casework for you! You know that brand-new flower shop – the Flower Basket? I talked to the owner when I ordered our anniversary flowers there. I went in again this morning to buy my undeserving wife some flowers! And Mrs Perry, who owns the shop, told me she was looking for an assistant; part-time. No special floristry work, just wrapping flowers, taking orders. I thought of Laura McCade and I went to see her. She not only said she thought she could do the job, but she showed a stirring of enthusiasm for it – that's *really* good! Mrs Perry rang a little while ago, and said she'd be pleased to have Miss McCade. It's going to do Laura a world of good!'

'Oh, David, bless you!' I murmured happily.

He looked very pleased with himself, when I looked up at him.

'How much do I get as your apprentice?' he demanded.

I kissed him.

'Will that do?' I asked.

'Mm.' He nodded, looking pleased. 'Between us, we've had quite a day, you and I, Mrs Pembury!'

CHAPTER 6

Sally Allister's son was born on the last day of April. Sally's husband, Douglas, telephoned the good news to David and me as we were breakfasting, before David began his morning surgery.

We were delighted, of course. Sally was an old friend of ours, and had been bridesmaid at our wedding.

'I can see her this afternoon,' I told David. 'I'll ring up the Flower Basket and ask them for the stork!'

David looked at me with an amused twinkle in his eyes.

'Seems to me the stork has already called on Sally!' he retorted drily.

'Idiot! They have a basket shaped like a stork at the flower shop, and if you want to send flowers to brand-new mums, they'll arrange them in this basket – and collect it after the flowers are over. A nice idea, I think! I'm so pleased for her, David! Doug said that Sally's father is already talking about his grandson being able to take over the running of the store one day!'

David put his hand over mine in a gesture of perfect understanding – the kind that has made our marriage so wonderful; he knew what I was thinking.

'All right, darling!' he said gently. 'When it's *our* turn, we'll surprise them all. Triplets, perhaps!'

He kissed me very satisfactorily. I cleared away the breakfast dishes, thinking about Sally. Then I prepared David's surgery and checked over the waiting-room. It wasn't the kind of day for a full waiting-room: blue sky, sunshine, birds singing and the garden bright with daffodils.

I remembered the time when I had thought that Sally was going to marry David; in those days I had *hated* Dr David Pembury, because I mistook common sense for callousness and shyness for arrogance. Nowadays, whenever David wanted to tease me about our first meeting he murmured wickedly that hatred was akin to love.

As I expected, David had a quiet morning; after lunch, I drove to the Flower Basket and collected my present for Sally. Laura

McCade handed over the stork basket with its bright cargo of spring flowers; she was an ex-patient of mine, and I felt a great uplift of thankfulness to see Laura settling so well into her new job; her eyesight had forced her to give up working at dressmaking.

Laura had once worked at Carmichael's, and she handed me a big bunch of violets, tied with ribbons.

'For Mrs Allister,' she said. 'I'm so pleased about the baby!'

'And you, Laura?' I asked. 'How are things with you?'

She knew what I meant.

'Oh, it isn't easy!' she admitted. 'But I like this job; no one could be miserable for long, working amongst flowers! And I won't need to take in students, now!'

At the maternity home, I was greeted by a radiant Sally. The baby, small and red-faced, had the crumpled look of all new babies; but I never ceased to marvel at the perfection in miniature that is a new baby.

'William Douglas Allister,' Sally told me proudly. 'Doug and I have earmarked you and David for godparents, Julie. Hope you don't mind...'

I spent a very happy afternoon with Sally. I went home, eager to tell David about it, but he had been delayed by an emergency, and telephoned to tell me that he would be late for evening surgery.

I set about preparing everything for him. I had almost finished when I heard an agitated tapping at the outer surgery door.

I knew that kind of knocking – doctors and nurses develop some kind of sixth sense about it, I think. I had an emergency – on the doorstep.

When I opened the door two girls of about fifteen stood there. It was quite obvious that the casualty was the taller of the two, an attractive girl with cropped dark hair, dressed in a bright-coloured shirt and jeans. The jeans were torn at one knee, and blood oozed from a cut; there was dirt on her face, another small cut on her chin – and she looked as though she was going to burst into tears.

The other girl explained:

'June came off her bicycle – a silly old man stepped off the pavement without looking where he was going! We saw this was a doctor's, so I thought–'

'Come in!' I said.

I took them into David's surgery. The cut on June's knee was fairly deep, but it would heal quickly, on good young flesh. I bathed it and dressed it, examined the cut on her chin and put a square of plaster over it. I offered June a cup of tea, for she still seemed shocked and dazed, but she shook her head.

'Well,' I said cheerfully, 'your mother is

going to wonder what you've been doing, when you walk indoors tonight!'

An odd look crossed June's face; but she half-smiled, though with an effort. The other girl, whose name was Hilary, said she would retrieve their bicycles – which were not damaged – and see June safely home.

They both thanked me for what I had done. Of the two, I thought, June was the more reserved. I saw them on their way, and there was an end of the matter, I believed – although a nurse's training teaches one to be methodical, and, just for the record, I had made a note of June's full name and address, and the treatment I had given her.

June Whitton, Nineteen Curtis Road. I knew where it was: a road of big, old-fashioned houses, most of them divided into flats, on the outskirts of the town.

An unexpected caller arrived about a week later; it was a glorious afternoon, and I was busy in the garden, when I heard the doorbell.

I opened the door to a slim young woman in a pink linen dress; her dark hair was short and curly, she had a casually attractive air about her. She was in her mid-thirties, I judged, and there was something vaguely familiar about her face, though I could not place her as one of David's patients.

'Are you Mrs Pembury?' she asked.

'Yes,' I said.

She held out the flowers she had been carrying; they had obviously been picked from a garden, and carefully and lovingly made into a posy.

'With my thanks for your help,' she said. A pause, and then she added:

'June Whitton is my daughter. She had an accident the other evening, and you were very kind...'

Of course! The resemblance to June was suddenly clear!

'This is kind!' I said, touched by the gesture. 'I only did what anyone else would have done. How is June?'

'Completely recovered!' Mrs Whitton assured me; but I sensed something not quite right – a hint of strain in the voice, a look of unhappiness in her eyes. David teases me about having an uncanny sense of *smell* for trouble, and I had a strong conviction that Mrs Whitton had something on her mind.

'Come and have a cup of tea,' I suggested. 'I've done enough gardening for one afternoon, and I'm just going to make myself a large pot of tea.'

Mrs Whitton hesitated for only a moment; then she smiled.

'Sounds wonderful,' she said. 'It *is* a beautiful day; I had a day's leave due to me, and I seem to have chosen the right time to take it!'

There is a little stone terrace, overlooking the garden, at the back of our house; a perfect suntrap. I put a chair beside mine, for June's mother, and went into the kitchen to prepare a tea-tray.

Mrs Whitton was eager to talk about June; and she did so with pride, when I came back with the tray.

'There was a time when I didn't think she'd get through her eleven-plus – she *hated* homework! But she's safely past *that* stage, I think! She's top of her form, and a prefect, and does well at games. She still isn't sure what she wants to be – last week it was a P.E. instructor! Oh, she isn't a paragon of virtue!' Mrs Whitton laughed, and looked ruefully at me. 'She spends all her pocket money on pop records, and sometimes I worry about the rather odd boys she brings home!'

'I expect most mothers do!' I told her. 'It's just a phase.'

'I know. I'm proud of her, really – she's a good girl. At least–'

There was a pause. Mrs Whitton's voice had wobbled over the last two words, and they didn't make sense to me: *at least…?*

Puzzled, I looked at Mrs Whitton, and to my astonishment, I saw that her eyes were suspiciously bright. She twisted her handkerchief between her fingers, staring unblinkingly at the sky behind the trees at the bottom of the garden, as though willing herself to concentrate on something in order to prop up her slipping self-control.

Only it didn't work for her. To my dismay, her face crumpled and she suddenly burst into tears, putting her hands over her face and weeping so bitterly that I felt both horrified and helpless.

I let her cry, uninterrupted, because I felt she needed the release of tears.

When at last it was over, I poured her another cup of tea, and passed it across.

'What on earth must you think of me?' she said miserably.

'I think you're very worried about something,' I told her frankly. 'But I don't know whether you want to talk about it; usually it helps to talk.'

She said wearily:

'I doubt if *this* ever will sort itself out; but sometimes it's easier to talk to a near-stranger. I haven't any close relatives – my mother died a couple of years ago; and I'm not Mrs Whitton at all. I'm Miss Elisabeth Whitton, spinster,' she said, with a world of bitterness in her voice. 'June is my illegitimate daughter. Nearly sixteen years ago, I was going to be married, and then, a week before the wedding, Max told me he couldn't go through with it, because he had met someone else. It was a dreadful shock. So there was no wedding – and then I discovered that I was expecting June. I'm not making excuses for myself, Mrs Pembury.'

'June wasn't the result of a casual affair,' I pointed out gently, wanting to comfort her.

'No; but I should have *waited*. So easy to be wise, afterwards. I was nineteen and terribly in love with Max, but it was still wrong... Well, I moved away from my home-town, as soon as I knew; stayed with a wonderful old aunt of my mother's. I never considered having June adopted. I loved her for herself, and because she reminded me of Max. I was very lucky – for the first few years I had a living-in job as mother's help – and my own mother was wonderful. Then, when June began to grow up, I took secretarial training to get a better job, and we came to Ambersea. I've got a very good job, secretary to the head of the big wholesale firm on the Marlingham road ... everyone thinks I'm a widow, of course. When June was eleven, I legally adopted her, because I felt that would simplify matters. But I forgot that growing children ask all kinds of questions. June wants to know all about her father, and it's becoming more and more difficult to keep the truth from her. And then she began asking questions about my "wedding" – she said it was funny I had no photos of my wedding day – her friends' mothers all had them.

That was when I first realised she was suspicious. For the last few weeks, she has pestered me with questions – and hinted … only yesterday, she said that unmarried mothers only had themselves to blame, that they were selfish and didn't realise what misery they caused to their unwanted children!'

'That is a typical remark from a fifteen-year-old who hasn't yet had to face up to life and all its complexities,' I said.

'I know; but a difficult one to sidestep, under the circumstances,' Elisabeth Whitton replied candidly. 'I suppose I'm over-sensitive, but I feel that June is looking at me, asking herself what sort of woman her mother is…'

'She is bound to go on doing that until you tell her the truth,' I pointed out. 'If you just tell her what happened, simply and without any emotion, she'll have to accept it. Tell her to reserve her judgement on you until she finds herself in a similar situation one day – as well she may! I know that it sounds easy, in theory; in fact, it will be one of the hardest things you have ever had to do, but the longer you put it off, the worse it will be.'

'I know you're right,' Elisabeth admitted. 'I wish I could write her a letter – I'm so much better at explaining myself via pen and ink!'

'Then why not do just that – write her a letter?' I urged. 'Leave it in her room for her to read. Just the fact of telling her will make *you* feel better.'

She gave me an uncertain smile, reached in her handbag for her compact, and powdered her nose.

'You're right,' she said. 'I've got to do this – and soon. I think I feel worse even than when Max jilted me. It hasn't been easy to bring up June by myself, but I've felt it was worthwhile – I still do. I've tried not to be possessive; we've been good friends until recently. All right, Mrs Pembury – I'll take your advice, and put it all down on paper for June to read. And thank you for being such a sympathetic listener.'

I *should* be sympathetic, I told myself, after Elisabeth Whitton had left. I was so very lucky – to be married to David, to know a happiness that was almost perfect. I thought of Sally, at the maternity home, happily enjoying her loved and welcomed first baby; and I thought, with a sigh, of Elisabeth, for whom it had all been so different, fifteen years ago.

Of course I told David about it, when we were alone in the hour that belonged to us at the end of a doctor's busy day; he was sympathetic and understanding, as I had known he would be.

'Tell me, Julie,' he said quizzically. 'Why is

it that all the lame ducks seem to settle on *our* pond?'

I thought for a moment.

'Perhaps because it's such a nice pond,' I told him at last; and I think he knew what I meant.

If Elisabeth had been an old patient of mine, it would have been easy enough to have found an excuse to call on her; if she had been ill, I could have taken her some magazines. Miss Verney passed on to me the names of anyone old or ill or just lonely, who needed visitors, and this way, I felt I kept in touch with the outside world.

I had no real excuse to visit Elisabeth – and I *was* anxious to know how she was faring; she had seemed so lonely, and I knew how she dreaded telling June the truth, even by way of a letter.

'You don't need an excuse to visit June's mother,' David said, when I told him how I felt. 'There are times when a simple statement of fact is enough. Just tell her you wondered if there was anything you could do.'

I doubted that there was; however, I called on Elisabeth, one lovely May evening.

Elisabeth's was a ground floor flat. She came to the door wearing a print dress and sandals, so that, at first, she looked like June's elder sister – until I saw the strain, the unhappiness still in her face.

141

'Hello!' she said, sounding genuinely pleased to see me. 'Come in, and I'll return the hospitality of a pot of tea with a long, cool drink!'

The flat reflected her home-making talents; nothing in it was very modern or expensive, but oak had been lovingly polished, chintzes were fresh and crisp, there were books and flowers; pictures on the walls, a large framed photo of June in school uniform on the piano. The big sitting-room led directly into a cool, old-fashioned garden.

We sat by the open french windows, and I said bluntly:

'I've been wondering how things were – and if you had told June…'

'Yes – I wrote her a letter!' Elisabeth's smile was bitter, her chin went up with a pathetic air of defiance; she was trying so hard to pretend she didn't care, that she could weather this storm.

'I'm glad I told her,' Elisabeth added, 'because it had to be done. I don't quite know what reaction I expected. An air of condemnation, certainly – fifteen can be such a righteous age! But it's silent contempt – she makes me feel so worthless. It's her martyred attitude, too – it's *my* fault that she isn't like the other girls in her class, and she isn't going to let me forget it. I'm a – a kind of *Jezebel*, according to my daughter!

She said she never wanted me to refer to the letter again – not that *she* can ever forget it!'

'High drama,' I told her. 'That's something else that Miss Fifteen loves. Everything is larger than lifesize, blacker than black or whiter than white, to a girl of her age.'

'I know!' Elisabeth sighed. 'She'll get over it, and we'll be good friends again – I *hope*. Perhaps I'm expecting too much, too soon. We're terribly busy at the office, and I'm tired; that doesn't help.'

She seemed almost at the end of her tether, I thought worriedly. I suggested she needed a holiday, but she shook her head.

'I want to decorate the flat during my holiday. June wants me to let her make up a foursome, with another boy and girl, and go camping with her current boyfriend. I don't like him, and in any case, I told her I think she's too young. We had a scene about *that*, I'm afraid!'

There was nothing I could do but listen, although I think Elisabeth was glad just to talk to someone. June came in as I was leaving. She had been playing tennis and looked tanned and pretty in white shorts and shirt.

'Hello!' She seemed slightly taken aback at seeing me there.

'How are you?' I asked.

'Oh, fine!' she said, in a rather bored voice.

'I'd no idea you were a friend of Mother's.' She turned to her mother. 'I'm changing and going back to the Tennis Club. Rick's brother has some new records, and we're having a dance. Rick's waiting for me; I won't be in until late.'

'By ten, please,' Elisabeth said firmly. 'And what about your homework, June?'

'Oh, that! I'll get up an hour earlier in the morning and do it – don't make such a fuss! And that ten o'clock curfew really is the end! No one else has to be in that early. I can't promise to make it, either – I'm not going to look a fool in front of Rick! I can't see why *you* want me such a little goody!'

I was horrified; it was the most deliberate, calculated piece of insolence I had ever heard. June, I thought angrily, wanted a good, sound spanking!

'Why, June!' Elisabeth said calmly, 'I'm getting quite used to rudeness from you – but in front of guests, this is something new! Or perhaps I see so few people that you tend to forget your manners?'

I silently applauded Elisabeth. The shot went home – June coloured angrily, and stormed upstairs without a word, slamming her bedroom door behind her. June's behaviour was outrageous, I thought.

A few days later, David and I had a rare treat – an evening out together. We booked a window-table at the Fig Tree, an attractive restaurant on the sea-front. Ambersea was beginning to fill up with summer visitors and we were lucky to have a window-table at such short notice.

Two people came in and sat down at the next table. I recognised the girl – hard-looking, she was too young to be wearing so much make-up; she was mini-skirted and walked with a kind of insolent elegance that might have been attractive in a woman ten years older.

'That's June Whitton,' I told David.

He took a good look at her.

'Hm. A handful, I'd say. I don't care for her escort, either.'

Neither did I. He had an assumed air of arrogance, very long hair, a familiar casualness that I did not like, towards June. They ordered a meal and a bottle of wine; June was drinking her second glass of wine before she saw me.

She looked momentarily startled; then she tossed her head, gave me a look that told me plainly to mind my own business and turned all her attention to the boy with her whom she called 'Rick'. She laughed and showed off a good deal. They finished their meal and the bottle of wine, and left the restaurant together noisily, Rick with his arm around June's shoulders.

Poor Elisabeth, I thought compassionately.

Later, as David and I drove home, we saw a sports car parked along the far end of the sea-front. I had no difficulty in recognising the girl in Rick's arms – the moonlight, making a sparkling path of silver across the water picked out June quite clearly.

'It isn't any of our business, you know, darling,' David reminded me gently.

'I wasn't going to tell Elisabeth anyway,' I told him. 'She has enough to worry about.'

But it was Elisabeth, after all, who told me, when we met, shopping, one Saturday morning. She looked thinner and more exhausted than ever, as though she found life a hopeless problem that she could no longer tackle.

'June goes everywhere with Rick Andrews,' she told me. 'He's twenty, he's got too much money and too few principles, I'd say, from the little I've seen of him. He's taken June to the Fig Tree once or twice, and June had been drinking too much last time he brought her home. I gave them both a piece of my mind. Rick thought it was very funny. June is furious with me – she says I haven't run *my* life so well that I can afford to dictate as to how she runs hers. Her school work is suffering, and she's lost her prefect's badge; she doesn't seem to care.'

'You need to get away from it all, for a while,' I urged.

She pushed a hand wearily through her hair.

'I haven't been sleeping well – I lie awake and worry about June. And things don't seem to ease up at the office,' she admitted.

A few days after my meeting with June, Miss Verney telephoned and asked if I'd like to visit a patient of Nurse Connolly's, an old lady living alone in Perrymouth Gardens. I took some books and spent a pleasant hour with the old lady, on an evening when David had no surgery. Perrymouth Gardens led from Curtis Road, so I drove down to Number Nineteen at the end of my visit, to see how Elisabeth was getting on.

I rang the bell twice before it was answered. There was a sports car parked at the kerb. June opened the door, indolently, and eyed me as though I had no business there.

Her crumpled mini-skirt was one of the shortest I have ever seen; she wasn't wearing shoes, her hair was dishevelled, and her lipstick smudged. The rumpled look was so obvious that my eyebrows went up.

She said sulkily: 'Mother's working late. I don't know when she'll be back.' She saw my raised eyebrows, and smiled, an impudent, contemptuous smile.

'Did Mother send you along to see if I was behaving myself?' she asked; and I heard Rick Andrews snigger, somewhere in the background. I remembered that Elisabeth had forbidden him to come to the flat.

I know I lose my temper much too easily – and sometimes it isn't justified. This is one of the times I *don't* regret losing it!

'Your mother didn't send me,' I retorted. 'I imagine she wouldn't want to bother to go to such lengths for a daughter who obviously isn't worth it – for someone who's making herself so cheap and easy to get. However, that's your affair. It's your mother I'm concerned with! Oh yes, I know all about your feeling martyred and badly treated because your mother and father weren't married! Your mother loved your father and hoped to marry him. She didn't have you as the result of a casual affair, though by the way you behave, she might well have done!'

I hadn't meant to imply that June might indulge in the kind of casual affair that could result in a baby; but when I saw the look on her face and the colour in her cheeks, I suddenly realised that Rick was trying to persuade her into such an affair.

'What I do is none of your business!' she cried.

'Thank heavens!' I retorted. 'I wonder if you're worth all your mother did for you? The years of working for two people, bringing you up alone, coping without a father? I doubt it. You're fifteen! Wait until you know more about life before you act so high and mightily, and sit in judgement on other people! I *wish* your mother had been married – to the kind of man who would have made sure you came in at the proper time and didn't entertain the wrong sort of people in his home! *That* would have done you good! Why don't you look at yourself and see what sort of person *you* are becoming instead of being so busy punishing your mother?'

I marched back to the car, and drove home, still furious. I told David, of course; he shook his head at me in mock dismay.

'It probably did *you* good to say what you thought – though I doubt if it will have any effect on June,' he told me.

I had to agree with him. A couple of weeks later, Elisabeth called at the surgery with some flowers for me. She was in a hurry, and couldn't stay, but told me that June had given up Rick Andrews. She said nothing about my visit to the house, so obviously June hadn't mentioned it. I was frankly very worried about Elisabeth, and told her she should see her own doctor. She smiled and shook her head.

'It's the heat, and all the extra work,' she said vaguely. 'I'm getting too old to cope with it all!'

She tried to joke, but it failed dismally.

David had to make an emergency call to

one of his patients at the end of evening surgery, a few days later. I tidied surgery and waiting-room, filed away the patients' record cards, and was thinking longingly about supper on the terrace, when there was an agitated tapping at the door. I hoped it was something I could cope with as I had coped with June's cut knee. Certainly I didn't expect to see June herself standing there.

Her face, devoid of make-up, was the scared face of a child.

'Is my mother here?' she asked uncertainly. 'I can't find her. She should have been home three hours ago. I rang the man she works for, at his home, and he said she hadn't been to the office all day! I tried a couple of friends, but they haven't seen her. Then I thought of you!'

'Oh?' I said shortly. 'It's quite a change for *you* to be concerned about your mother's whereabouts! I should imagine she's got tired of coping with you, and left you to your own devices.'

David said, afterwards, that I shouldn't have said that to her; it was stinging and unkind. But I felt she deserved it.

'Come in!' I added. 'We'd better begin by checking any other places to which she might have gone; then we can try the police and the hospitals.'

June went very white. I saw how her hands

150

shook, and she looked as though she was going to cry. She wasn't so grown-up as she pretended to be, faced with a situation of this kind.

I spent half an hour telephoning. At least Elisabeth hadn't met with an accident, for I drew blank at the local hospitals. I saw some of the tension go out of June.

'The best thing you can do,' I said crisply, 'is to go home and wait there for your mother.'

'Will you come with me?' she asked, in a small voice.

I left a note for David, and drove her to Curtis Road.

The flat seemed unnaturally empty and tidy – June must have felt the emptiness, for she burst into tears as we stepped inside.

'Suppose she never comes back!' she said bitterly.

'Of course she will!' I said, trying to sound convincing.

June sat down on the settee, still crying.

'You don't understand; nobody ever understands!' she cried.

The heart-cry of fifteen, I thought, feeling sorry for her.

'You made her feel that what she had done was cheap and contemptible!' I pointed out calmly. 'But perhaps you've discovered for yourself how easy it is to say "yes" instead of "no" to someone you care about. She loved you, June; she spent years trying to make a happy home for you, to give you everything she could, to help and encourage you. The fact that she didn't have a wedding ring doesn't make her less of a fine person. She's been a wonderful mother.'

'I know!' June whispered forlornly. 'Only it seemed awful, not having a father, and a mother who wasn't married, and hoping no one would find out at school, and I told Rick because I thought he'd understand ... he laughed and thought it was funny, and when I gave him up, he said he was going to tell everyone.'

'He won't tell anyone, probably,' I pointed out. 'People wouldn't think much of him for saying such a thing, anyway – and he's not so big and sophisticated as he likes to think!'

'I don't care what he does,' June said miserably, 'so long as Mum comes back. It seems so – so *dead*, without her. She used to laugh a lot, and sometimes when she was happy she played the piano, and we used to go shopping together. I wish it could be like it used to be! I know I was horrible to her because I thought what she did was dreadful, but everybody does something that's wrong, sometimes and some people have to pay for it more than others...'

I let her talk. She was learning to reason it out for herself, groping towards the realisation that no one is perfect.

152

When her tears were over, she announced her intention of making some tea. I was beginning to be worried, myself, but as June went towards the kitchen, a car drew up at the kerb. Not a red sports car – a sedate and far-from-new black saloon. The driver was a pleasant-looking man about Elisabeth's age. Carefully he helped a weary-looking woman from the car.

'June!' I called. 'Your mother is home!'

Her relief was joy to see. It was obvious just how much she cared for her mother under that hard little shell of hers. She opened the door with impatient fingers; she had learnt the special kind of anxiety that comes from waiting for someone who doesn't come home at the expected time.

'Mum! Where have you been? I was so worried!' she cried.

The man with Elisabeth stepped into the hall, still holding her arm. I liked his face – clear-cut, good-humoured; I liked the reassuring smile he gave June.

'Your mother almost stepped under my car, at the park gates, a little while ago. I gave her a cup of coffee, and decided it might be a good idea to bring her home before she did it to someone whose brakes aren't as good as mine!'

His touch of humour relieved the strain, just a little. Elisabeth murmured vaguely that she was so tired, she had just been

153

walking and thinking all day. I saw June look ashamed, as she helped her mother to a chair.

It was time to go, I felt. Time for June to take over. Already she was very capably coping with the situation, offering tea to the man who had brought her mother home, and thanking him. Elisabeth was looking at her daughter as though she couldn't believe what was happening, but some of the distraught look had gone from her face. June had been badly frightened; I had the feeling that some good might come of it.

'I'm so tired,' Elisabeth murmured, still vague, as though everything was unreal.

'Bed for you, as soon as you've had some tea and something to eat,' June said briskly.

'She'll make it,' said the man who had brought Elisabeth home, as we closed the front door behind me. He smiled at my bewilderment.

'I mean the daughter – not her mother! It's not hard to understand what's happened – she's been giving her mother a tough time of it, because of her own growing pains, and now she's been brought up with a jolt. I've got a daughter of ten – I'm a widower. Don't know what *I'll* do when Mandy gets to be a teenager!'

I liked him – for his perceptivity, his understanding. He told me that his name was John Blythe. We went our separate

154

ways, and I arrived home at the same time as David.

I wondered often how Elisabeth and her daughter were faring; but I took David's advice, and left them alone – until the day I came back from shopping for a special present for Sally's baby. It was teatime, and David was just back from his afternoon rounds.

'I've had a visitor,' he told me. 'She came with an invitation for you to go and have supper at Number Nineteen Curtis Road tomorrow evening. Such a nice child. Most interested in medicine, she said; wanted to know all about a doctor's life. We had quite a long chat. You missed her by minutes.'

June answered the door to me the following evening. She was wearing a businesslike smock and gave me a friendly smile.

'Come in, Mrs Pembury! Mother's having a rest upstairs – I've told her she ought to do that, every evening, when she comes home. I've got supper all ready to take out into the garden.'

'How is your mother?' I asked cautiously.

'Improving. She doesn't eat enough, and I'm trying to see that she does!' June said, with a deliciously bossy air. 'Anyway, Mother has a boy-friend and it's good for her; Mr Blythe has certainly made a difference to her. He called the day after he

155

brought her home, and took her for a drive. She's going to a show with him next week, and she's quite excited about it. She *should* have some interest outside the home and the office, you know.'

'Yes,' I agreed solemnly, stifling a wild desire to laugh; and feeling a great thankfulness for the old June, come out of the shell, the lovable, thoughtful person too long tucked away out of sight.

'*I* don't want boy-friends, Mrs Pembury,' June added solemnly. '*I've* got other, more important things to think about. I – well, I've been neglecting my school work recently, and I want to catch up. I'll have to study hard if I mean to be a doctor, won't I? And that's what I want to be, more than anything else – a doctor. Like Dr Pembury!' She blushed and smiled. 'I think he's absolutely wonderful. When I called yesterday he told me about his work, and that's when I knew what I was meant to be,' she told me, with a dreamy, faraway look in her eyes.

It was a happy evening – Elisabeth so relaxed, June fussing over her mother. I went home feeling very happy, to find David dozing over a book.

I knelt beside his chair, thoroughly enjoying myself.

'Darling, you've made such a conquest, I'm jealous!'

'What on earth do you mean?' he demanded.

'June thinks you're wonderful. She wants to be a doctor just like you! She's been asking me about you all the evening just because she loves to hear me talk about you. I didn't realise you had so much charm, darling! I'll have to look to my laurels!' I teased wickedly.

David put down his book and grabbed hold of me.

'That'll do!' he retorted. 'In six months' time, she'll probably meet an actor, and want to be an actress; and if you think you're going to have fun in the meantime, teasing me – you aren't! I shall take disciplinary action against you!' He chuckled. 'Anyway,' he added, looking down at me thoughtfully, 'don't *you* think I'm wonderful?'

'You know perfectly well that I do!' I retorted.

CHAPTER 7

Sally and Douglas Allister's baby son, William Douglas, was christened on a glorious June afternoon, when every garden in Ambersea seemed to be bursting at the seams with flowers, and the warmth of the sun soaked right down into one's bones.

I was sorry when it was over. David and I had to leave early, as he had an evening surgery. He squeezed my hand as we got into the car, waving our goodbyes.

'Remember, darling,' he whispered, 'that when it's our turn, we'll really surprise them, and have triplets!'

But when would it be our turn? I sighed – both David and I longed to become a real family.

'Nothing less than quads!' I retorted gaily.

It was a busy surgery that evening; I knew many of the patients from my district nursing days, and it was like renewing old friendships to see them again.

One of David's patients was Katherine Kendle, a happy-go-lucky woman in her mid-thirties, plump and dark and pretty. I had met her once or twice at Delia Fairfield's. Since Delia, bored and unhappy, had found herself a niche working beside her husband – and had become a different person in consequence – Mrs Kendle had gone to the Fairfield house for a few hours each day to do light housework.

Katherine had an adopted daughter, ten-year-old Maureen. It was Katherine's one sorrow in life that she and Derek could not have children. But they were both very proud of Maureen, who was so like

Katherine that no one would have guessed she was adopted. Maureen had the same cheerful temperament and dark prettiness.

Yet, that evening, Maureen seemed withdrawn and quiet; by contrast, her mother had a warm luminous look of contentment about her. If I hadn't known that she was unable to have children, I'd have suspected that she was going to have the baby she and her husband had wanted so much.

Miracles do happen. David's examination confirmed that Mrs Kendle *was* going to have a baby! She was so delighted that I thought she was going to throw her arms around David's neck and kiss him – not that I would have blamed her!

David knew how she felt. Over supper, as we relaxed contentedly on the terrace, enjoying the warm, scented summer air, he said:

'It's such a joy to be able to give a patient good news – not just reassurance, but really exciting news. That's one of the things I enjoy about being a doctor.'

'You're thinking about Katherine Kendle, aren't you?' I said.

'Yes, darling. Babies seem to be in the air today, don't they? The look on Mrs Kendle's face put the finishing touch to my day!'

'Mm.' I frowned at him. 'Did you see Maureen, though? I thought she looked –

oh, remote, somehow, and out of tune with the world.'

'Does she know she's adopted?' David asked thoughtfully.

'Oh yes. Katherine says she and Derek have never made any secret of that fact – very sensible of them. In fact, Katherine told Maureen that adopted means being "very specially chosen." A lovely way of putting it, I think.'

'Well, even ordinary children sometimes feel a twinge or two of jealousy about an addition to the family,' David pointed out. 'Though I'll admit it usually shows itself when the baby has actually arrived. After all, this one can't have much reality, yet, for Maureen. We're assuming, of course, that Katherine has told Maureen that she thinks she's having a baby.' He smiled at me. 'I see the look in your eye, Julie! Stop worrying about Maureen Kendle. Maybe she'd eaten too much ice-cream, or had extra home-work, and that accounted for her quietness – nothing to do with the baby!'

David laughed; his mood was teasing and light-hearted, and I hoped he was right. He often says I am a born meddler, who loves trying to put the world right – and he forgets that one of my biggest reasons for meddling is the fact that I'm so happy with him I feel I just have to spread some of it around, if I can!

As it happened, David was wrong about Maureen. A few days later, I met Katherine and I was shocked to see how drawn and worried she looked. She was standing outside Ambersea's newest tea-rooms, and managed a rather tired smile when she saw me.

'Come in and have a cup of coffee,' I said. 'You look as though you need one.'

Her eyes filled with tears.

'Coffee first,' I said firmly. 'And you can talk afterwards – *if* you feel like talking.'

'Talking won't make much difference to my problem,' she replied wearily; but when she had finished her coffee, she began to talk as though the words would not be damned up any longer.

'It's Maureen – she's *annoyed* about the baby – *if* that's the right word! And it doesn't make sense, because she was so pleased when I first told her that it was just possible she might have a brother or sister. I suspected, you see, Mrs Pembury, before I came to see your husband – oh, I was *sure!* Derek and I were like a couple of kids. We told Maureen that she could choose a name for the baby, and you should have seen her – so excited; and then, the day I came round to see your husband, she seemed to change completely. She was quiet when she came home from school; she wouldn't tell me what was wrong. When I said I knew for

161

certain that there was going to be a baby because Dr Pembury had said so, she said *she* didn't want a baby around the house. I was so surprised I didn't know what to say! Ever since then she has been as difficult as she can be – sulky, bored if we talk about the baby, behaving as though she didn't like us at all. I've questioned her, but she won't say what has made her change her mind. She's become so secretive – and she was never a secretive child, Mrs Pembury.'

Two tears rolled down in the direction of the empty coffee cup. I felt so sorry for Katherine – all her newfound joy suddenly dimmed, as though a light that had shone brightly had been put out.

'Children's minds work in the most extraordinary ways,' I told her. 'Though I can't imagine why she was so pleased at first, and is now so hostile about it. Someone must have said something to her, about being adopted.'

Katherine shook her head.

'I've done everything I can think of to reassure her, tell her she will mean as much to us as she always did, and that we need and want her. Another thing: Derek was going to redecorate her bedroom for her during the school holidays, and I've promised her new curtains and a "grown-up" bedspread to match. She told us not to bother! Did you ever hear anything so

162

absurd? Derek has been patient with her, but I'm afraid he's beginning to be annoyed with her, now.'

I understood. Derek's concern, at the moment, was for his wife.

I felt helpless. I told David about it, that evening.

'I don't know what has made Maureen change her mind about the baby,' he admitted. 'It seems odd; as you say, someone *must* have said something to her. But then she has always known she was adopted. *I* don't know, love.' He smiled and shook his head. 'There's nothing we can do,' he told me gently.

The following week Katherine brought Maureen to the surgery. Maureen had insisted on staying home from school, saying she felt sick; she also seemed to have several rather mysterious aches and pains. I watched while David made a routine examination and talked to her. I had never seen a child look so forlorn and miserable, and it made me uneasy.

I looked at Katherine; nothing but concern on her face, and in her whole manner. The Kendles had been good parents.

I remembered, vividly, my unexpected meeting with Delia Fairfield that morning – a cheerful, happy Delia, who greeted me like an old friend, and asked me if Miss Verney had asked for my help in the Summer Fair.

The Summer Fair was Miss Verney's good deed – it raised money to buy comforts for elderly patients, and those outside the scope of the usual welfare services. I told Delia that I was going to call on Miss Verney in a few days' time; and then Delia told me how sorry she was to lose Mrs Kendle.

'...such a cheerful person, Mrs Pembury. Even if she hadn't been such a splendid worker, her cheerfulness would have compensated for everything! I understand she's going to have a baby, and she's delighted, naturally. They wanted a big family you know. I remember when they adopted Maureen from the Children's Home. Such a happy baby – and such a nice child. They say parents get the children they deserve...'

David's voice brought me back to earth. I showed Maureen and her mother out, and brought in the next patient. We had no chance to talk until we were having supper together that evening.

'Maureen seems perfectly healthy, so far as I can tell from a routine examination,' David said. 'If there's nothing physically wrong, then it would seem she needs some kind of psychological treatment.'

'Oh no!' I protested quickly. Then I remembered the sullen look of unhappiness on Maureen's face, and sighed. Perhaps

164

David was right, and expert help was needed to unravel the tangles in her emotions.

On my way to see Miss Verney, a few days later, I suddenly remembered that Lorraine Allison went to the same school as Maureen, and they were probably classmates.

It was a school holiday, and Lorraine was just off to the beach with Shirley and Sandra. I handed Shirley a pile of magazines, told Sandra Miss Verney would probably be pleased to have some help from her on the day of the Fair (Sandy loved to feel useful!) and steered the conversation casually towards school, asking how Lorraine was getting on with art, for which she showed quite a talent. It wasn't difficult, then, to bring Maureen into the conversation.

'Maureen's in trouble with everyone at school,' Lorraine told me, with a virtuous air of being on the outside that rather amused me. 'She doesn't want to do anything, not even games, and she used to like games ever so much! And she won't talk to anybody or be friendly. I think she's *silly!*'

I thought over Lorraine's words, on my way to see Miss Verney. The memory of that small, unhappy face bothered me. Maureen had looked *old*, I reflected, puzzled. As though she was trying to cope with something that was beyond her.

The day was very hot; the sky was a deep, brilliant blue, with not the merest hint of a thistledown cloud on the horizon. The air seemed to be standing still, holding its breath; I drove along the sea-front, past a beach packed with holiday-makers, and thought how lucky we were to live by the sea all the year – David and I sometimes managed to get down for a swim in the evenings.

I was glad there was no evening surgery. I would be able to dawdle over tea and Miss Verney – who loved the sun – was sure to have it in the garden.

I was right; tea was set out beneath one of the pear trees that grew in the big grounds.

'Cucumber sandwiches, strawberries and cream,' Miss Verney said, with immense satisfaction. 'Reminds me of garden parties. These are almost the last of the strawberries, though. July, already! And the Summer Fair a month away! I know we can count on you...'

'Of course!' I said quickly; but I felt tired, mentally as well as physically weary, as I sat listening to Miss Verney's plans for the Fair. Perhaps David was right when he had insisted that I was doing too much.

Only last night he had taken me in his arms and said gently:

'Julie, you're looking weary. Could be the

long, hot summer.'

'It's just the same for you,' I had pointed out. 'You're as busy as ever. We're due for two weeks' holiday in mid-September, anyway – remember?'

'That's a long way off. Julie, I could get a surgery nurse; that would leave you free to look after the house, instead of doing two jobs.'

'Are you trying to tell me I'm dismissed?' I had retorted indignantly. 'I *like* being surgery nurse – it means I can meet people and talk to them, and share a bigger part of your life. I refuse to leave, Dr Pembury!'

David's answer had been a long and very satisfactory kiss; but I knew he was still convinced I was overdoing things...

With an effort, I pulled back my wandering thoughts and listened to Miss Verney.

I stayed longer than I meant to in the peaceful, secluded garden. As I walked back into the house with Miss Verney, Barbara Connolly arrived from her afternoon round. Seeing her carried me back to my first day of district nursing; I remembered how cheerful and reassuring she had been.

'Busy day?' I asked sympathetically.

'Not too bad. This long, sunny spell seems to be giving everyone a new lease of life. As a matter of fact, I'd have finished earlier than this, but I had an S.O.S.' She turned to

Miss Verney and explained:

'I was giving Mrs Sayers her injection, when there was a knock on the kitchen wall. As soon as I had finished, Mrs Sayers went into the house next door. She came back for me; she was worried, because her neighbour was feeling very unwell. I went in, but there wasn't anything I could do; she was a nice little soul, expecting a baby in a few months. She's terrified of losing the baby – anyway, it was a false alarm.'

I knew Mrs Sayers; she lived in Kilmartin Grove. And Mrs Kendle also lived in Kilmartin Grove.

'Mrs Kendle,' I said aloud.

Barbara nodded.

'That's right. Number Seventeen. She seemed to have something on her mind!' She grinned at me. 'Problems are your department, aren't they, Julie? Anyway, it was half-past five when I left, and Mrs Kendle was frantic because her daughter should have been home from school an hour ago. She said her husband was due home, so I told her to let him cope. You know what children are – especially on summer evenings...!'

I didn't share Barbara's happy-go-lucky state of mind; but then, I reminded myself, Barbara knew nothing of Maureen's odd behaviour recently.

I looked at my watch; half past six. David

would not be home until after seven. I said goodbye to Barbara and Miss Verney, and on an impulse I drove straight to Kilmartin Grove. Probably, by now, Maureen has come home, I told myself; I'm worrying about nothing, just as Katherine Kendle has been doing.

But when I knocked at the door of the neat little semi-detached with the pretty garden, where the Kendles lived, the door was opened quickly, and at once, as though the people inside were waiting for a knock, a caller...

I guessed that the harassed-looking man with the rumpled dark hair was Derek Kendle, although I had never met him. He looked exasperated, tired and extremely worried. Mrs Kendle came from the back to the hall, and I could see she had been crying.

'Come in, Mrs Pembury,' she said. She introduced me to Derek, and explained:

'We're worried. Maureen hasn't come home. Derek has been to the park and he looked in at the fun-fair – we used to take her there, and she loved it. We don't know what to do... Derek went round to her form-mistress and she said that Maureen hadn't been to school this afternoon.'

She began to cry. I took her into the living-room, and made her sit down.

'I'm furious with Maureen for worrying her mother like this!' Derek exploded.

Katherine put out a hand and held his tightly for a moment, in a gesture that I understood. She looked at me, and asked me if I would pour tea for them all; then she went upstairs to Maureen's room, and Derek walked over to the window, staring at the garden, his shoulders hunched despairingly. There was nothing I could say to comfort him, I thought miserably.

'I shall have to tell the police,' he said, finally. 'Children ... one hears such things, nowadays; and always, we feel: oh, it couldn't happen to us. But it could...'

'Don't think like that!' I said quickly; but his uneasiness had communicated itself to me, and I *wondered* ... Maureen didn't have a long walk to school. There was a school warden at the main road ... if there had been an accident, they would have known by now.

Katherine came downstairs very slowly; when she spoke, her voice was quiet, completely calm.

'I've just made a thorough search of her room,' she said. 'Her pyjamas have gone, and a couple of books that were her favourites. I picked up her china piggy bank. It's empty. She had about fifteen shillings in it. Oh, Derek!' Her calm crumpled suddenly, as he took her in his arms. 'She's run away. Why? What did we do to make her so unhappy?'

170

'Nothing, my love.' Gently he pushed back the thick hair from her face. 'It was because of the baby coming. She was jealous; and we thought she'd be pleased. She *was* pleased at first.' He looked at me over Katherine's shoulder, and added furiously:

'I've never spanked Maureen in my life, but when I find out where she is she'll have a spanking that she'll never forget.'

Katherine put her fingers against his lips.

'You know you don't mean it! And that's not the answer! We've got to find out what has made her do this.'

'I've told you what's wrong with her!' Derek snapped. 'Jealousy! Well, she just has to learn, that's all, that she isn't the only person in the world...'

His anger against his daughter was all on the surface, I realised; an outlet for his anxiety. Underneath, he was as worried about Maureen as Katherine was, wondering what had happened to her. I had a vivid mental image of a small, forlorn figure somewhere, with pyjamas and books, and the contents of a piggy bank – going *where?* Somehow, her world had fallen apart, and we were all helpless, unable to put it together again for her.

'I'm going down to the police station,' Derek said reluctantly. I saw the agony in Katherine's face; supposing it had been my daughter? I thought. Mine and David's...?

There was nothing I could do for Katherine. Mrs Sayers came in to be with her, while Derek went to the police station, and I went home to David.

'What's the matter, darling?' he asked concernedly, as soon as I stepped inside the house; he put out his arms, and I went straight into them. That's one of the things I love best about David – the way he holds out his arms to me, whenever he sees a certain look on my face.

I told him the story of Maureen's disappearance. He listened sympathetically.

'Derek Kendle has gone to the police, as you say,' he pointed out. 'I know what you're thinking, Julie – that Maureen may have come to harm. She has been missing quite a few hours; but, with the police looking for her, she has a better chance of being found quickly – before dark...'

Before dark ... I shivered. She was only ten years old, after all...

'Lorraine!' David said. 'You say she is in Maureen's class at school! I wonder if Maureen has said anything to her which would give us a clue?'

'I hadn't thought of that!' I said. 'Let's go, David!'

He drove me to the Allison home. Don't hope for too much, I told myself over and over again; it may be that Lorraine knows nothing at all.

I explained the situation to Shirley; Lorraine had just come in from play. I told her that Maureen was missing, and asked her if she had said anything about going away.

'Try to remember,' I begged. 'It's very important; we can't find her.'

Lorraine nodded. 'She *did* say something the other day about going back to the Home because that's where she lived when she was a baby,' Lorraine said finally.

'The Home?' I whispered. 'Of *course!* Why didn't we think of that? But surely, if she had been there, the Matron would have got in touch with someone by now. No, wait! I've just remembered, David. The Matron is new – Miss Carroll retired last month, and Miss Jordan only took over then... She wouldn't know Maureen.'

'We don't know that Maureen *is* there,' David pointed out. 'Don't be too hopeful until we're sure, darling. Let's go home and telephone.'

I am sure that David broke the speed limit, driving back. I don't remember very much, because I was excited and apprehensive and impatient, a medley of feelings that left me shaken and quite unlike the sensible person I usually am! Only David's calmness sustained me, as I raced indoors, and dialled the number of the Home. I felt his hand on my shoulder, steadying, comforting.

It seemed an age before I could get through to Miss Jordan; I realised the slenderness of the thread to which I clung. Relief was an anti-climax that left me feeling exhausted, when Miss Jordan said thankfully:

'Maureen Kendle? So *that's* her name! Yes, she fits your description; she came here more than an hour ago, with her books and pyjamas. Said she'd been adopted, as a baby, and wanted to come back here to live! In all my years of looking after children I've never come across such an extraordinary story!' Miss Jordan added ruefully. 'She wouldn't give me her name. Just asked if she could stay; said she had left home and had been in the park all the afternoon. I couldn't even get out of her what school she went to. I've been so worried; I tried to coax *some* information out of her, but she wouldn't say anything; I was about to telephone the police when you rang. Now why did she come here? Isn't she happy – or properly treated? She seemed to be well looked after, judging from her appearance...'

David, who had heard every word, took the telephone from me. He could see that I wasn't capable of saying anything at all. I was crying, tears of sheer relief.

Briskly, he explained the whole story to Miss Jordan, and asked her to keep Maureen there while he got in touch with the Kendles and arranged for her to be collected. Then he replaced the receiver, and said to me, with mock resignation:

'Off we go again, Mrs Pembury!'

'Oh, darling, I'm sorry!' I whispered contritely. 'Spoiling your evening off; making you dash all over the place...!'

He smiled down at me, wiping away the tears.

'I'll probably spend a lot of my spare time tagging along in the wake of your good deeds!' he retorted drily. 'It's all right by me – just so long as I can have my wife to myself *sometimes!*'

It was wonderful to be going to the Kendles with such good news, although I knew our troubles with Maureen were not yet over. As soon as Derek opened the door, he saw by my face that Maureen had been found.

I explained breathlessly to the Kendles where Maureen was; Katherine had no tears left to weep. She smiled tremulously, and held out her hand to Derek; and David said quietly:

'I would suggest, Mrs Kendle, that you let my wife fetch Maureen from the Home. It's important to find out *why* she went there, and she may talk more freely to someone outside her immediate family circle. One can't be *certain* that she will, of course; but it might be worth trying.'

Katherine hesitated and looked at Derek, who nodded.

'It seems to be a good idea,' he admitted. 'Mind you, her explanation had better be good. I'll go down to the station, and tell the police what has happened.'

I took the car and drove away. David said he would walk home, telling me that he felt in need of the exercise and fresh air!

Miss Jordan was vastly relieved to see me; she was a small, grey-haired woman, a warm and happy personality, obviously the kind of person a child would trust; though she admitted, with an air of defeat that she had been unable to get Maureen to talk to her.

'Maureen is in my office at the moment, she explained. 'I'll leave you to see her alone, Mrs Pembury, and not disturb you for a while. Perhaps you'll be able to find out what's wrong; I hope so. I don't like to see a child look so unhappy.'

When I went to Miss Jordan's office, Maureen was seated stiffly on the very edge of a chair. She glanced at me, and looked quickly away again. I saw how tightly she held her books, as though for comfort. She looked small and lonely and scared. I've *got* to reach her, I thought desperately.

'I've come to take you home,' I told her. 'Your mother and father are very worried about you, Maureen. They're upset, too, because they always thought you liked living with them.' I felt my way carefully, wondering if I was saying the wrong thing. 'You can't stay here, you know. This Home is for babies and children who haven't any family of their own; they're waiting for someone to come and choose them. You were lucky to be chosen to be part of a family; and now you don't want to be any more. Why?'

She fidgeted, and stared down at her books, while I held my breath. Then she said, with adult bitterness:

'You have to grow a baby yourself for it to be *really* yours. It's not the same if you just go and *choose* a baby.'

'Who told you this?' I asked, puzzled.

'Marilyn Foster. She's in my class at school. I knew where babies come from, anyway. My mother told me. But I didn't know that a baby didn't belong to you unless you grew it yourself. Marilyn's mother told her I was adopted, and Marilyn said that now my mother is having a baby it's different. They wouldn't have chosen me if they'd known they could grow one for themselves.'

'Oh yes, they would!' I retorted. 'They've had to wait a long time to grow this baby. It doesn't make any difference to mothers and fathers whether they grow babies or choose them! They love them just the same. Your mother and father want *you* just as much as the new baby that's coming. Why, Marilyn

Foster is the stupidest little girl I've ever heard of; she doesn't know *anything!*'

Maureen looked at me, half awed, half impressed, as though I had committed heresy. Clearly she had thought Marilyn Foster was an authority on the subject. I realised how much Marilyn's opinions had upset Maureen; but there was still something else. Maureen added reluctantly:

'It costs a lot of money to have a baby. I heard them saying so, one night when they thought I was in bed. They said they had given my pram and cot away and would have to buy new ones and there wouldn't be a holiday next year. So, as they won't need me when they've got a baby they grew all by themselves, I thought I might as well come back to the Home to live. *She* said something about me needing a school uniform next year, and getting me a bicycle for Christmas, and if I wasn't *there,* they wouldn't have to buy all those things as well as a cot and pram.'

Poor Maureen! Marilyn had planted the seeds and the idea had grown, vast and unhappy, too much for a ten-year-old mind to cope with. I longed to put my arms around Maureen and make a fuss of her, but I knew that would be useless at this moment.

'They've been looking everywhere for you,' I pointed out. 'They wouldn't have done that if they didn't love you and want

178

you back. They've had you all these years before the baby, so you've had much more love than him – or her.'

That was a new idea; I saw her thinking it over. Doubt struggled in her face with a longing to accept reassurance. Finally, she shook her head stubbornly.

'They'll never love me as much as their very own baby that they're growing. It can't ever be the same, Marilyn says!'

'Oh, bother Marilyn Foster!' I exploded, exasperated. 'I've never heard such nonsense in my life! Your mother and father don't really mind having to buy new things for the baby or a bicycle for you – it's part of being a family!' I drew a deep breath. 'You know, they ought to be very cross with you, because you've let them down, haven't you? They would never have decided to grow this baby if they hadn't thought they could count on you to help them with it!' I added, with sudden inspiration, telling myself that I was not really lying, only bending the truth a little!

'They thought you *wanted* a brother or sister!' I told her. 'They asked you to choose a name for it! And you ran away, just when they need you. They're having this baby as a special present for you, but you'll have to help look after it, and how can you do that if you're here, not at home, where you should be!'

I closed my eyes for a second, praying I had said the right thing. When I opened them, Maureen was looking at me warily. But, thankfully, I realised that the doubt and uncertainty had gone.

'Are they very cross with me?' she asked.

'No. Just sorry that you don't want to stay with them any more.'

'I *do* want to!' she whispered...

She sat very silent beside me as we drove back to Kilmartin Grove. The front door was wide open, and Derek waited there, his arms around Katherine. He looked at me, as though wondering what he should say and I said matter-of-factly:

'Maureen is sorry she has caused you all so much trouble.' Maureen ran to her mother, who put her arms around her daughter. We went into the house and I explained to them what Maureen had told me.

Katherine held her daughter tightly, and said contritely to me:

'I didn't realise she was thinking about the money angle. We can manage; it's just that we were talking over ways and means.'

'I don't need a bicycle,' Maureen said.

I looked at Derek. He rose splendidly to the occasion.

'We can manage the bicycle,' he said briskly. 'But it's no use buying you one if you aren't going to stay with us, is it?'

'I'm going to stay,' she promised.

He ruffled her hair.

'That's fine. As Mrs Pembury says, we wouldn't be having this baby if it wasn't that we thought you'd like a brother or sister; so we're going to need you to help look after it. We chose you because we wanted you very much; we're *always* going to want you, so no more listening to silly stories. And now, young lady, supper and bed for you...'

I drove home to David through the warm summer dusk, with a sense of gratitude for all the love that surrounded *me,* and a feeling that for once, I had *said* exactly the right thing!

Dearest David! As usual, he had a tray of tea waiting for me; as usual, he was ready to listen, while I sat in our big, comfortable living-room and re-told my story again. When I had finished he came over and put his hand under my chin, tilting my face up to his. '"Bending the truth" indeed! Julie Pembury, I *love* that bit!'

'It worked,' I said. 'That was the important thing!'

'I know.' He kissed me; then he put an arm around me and held me close in a quick, hard embrace. I knew that his thoughts were exactly the same as mine: how wonderful it would be to have a family of our own – even though they might cause us as much anxiety sometimes as Maureen had caused her parents!

CHAPTER 8

Whenever David and I had time to spare during the summer, we spent it on Amber-sea beach, swimming, lying in the sun and pretending we were holidaymakers.

We were lucky, David said, to have sand and sea all the year round. However, one golden August afternoon, we found a reasonably secluded part of the beach, and, after our swim, just lay there, soaking up the sun. David had, miraculously, managed a whole day off, and there was no surgery. I lay, blissfully content, thinking how lucky I was to have a husband like David.

David was trickling little rivulets of sand over my bare legs. I should have known it was all too good to be true – a doctor is never off duty. I realised that his attention had wandered, and he was looking at a girl who had just come from the water's edge.

I sat up and followed his glance. She was young, tanned and pretty; long-legged, with a marvellous figure, and blonde hair; about seventeen, I guessed; and she was limping badly, leaving blood with every footprint on the wet sand.

David was on his feet at once.

'Let me have a look!' he said, with an air of authority, as she approached.

Her face was puckered with pain, and she looked pale under her tan. David made her sit down and I saw the cut on her foot; it was long and deep.

'I stepped on a broken bottle,' she explained.

David has often expressed his opinion very forcibly as to what he would like to do with people who leave glass on the beach. He took his pocket handkerchief, and bound the cut tightly, but the blood still seeped through.

'I have a first aid kit in my car,' he told the girl. 'Just the same, I think that foot is going to need a stitch or two. I'll run you to the hospital.'

She had lovely dark blue eyes, long-lashed and clear, an attractive smile, tremulous at the moment, as she said:

'I'm awfully sorry. I don't want to be a nuisance. I'm sure it will be all right…'

'Nonsense!' said David. 'No trouble. You've got an extremely nasty cut there.' He smiled down at me. 'Go back to your sun-bathing, Julie. See you later.'

Resignedly, I lay back and closed my eyes. I dozed, lulled by the sun's warmth; when I awoke and glanced at my watch, I was astonished to see that David had been gone for more than an hour. The hospital was less than ten minutes' drive away. What on earth was keeping him? I wondered irritably. A pair of blue eyes, and a long fall of blonde hair?

I was being ridiculous, I told myself; but the afternoon had gone, and we would soon have to be going home.

I began gathering our things together, stowing them away into the beach bag. I had just finished when David came striding along the beach, looking very pleased with himself.

'Good thing I insisted on taking her to the hospital!' he said, 'That foot certainly needed a couple of stitches. And then I took her home. Darling, you'll never guess! She and her sister have rented Fisherman's Cottage for the summer.'

I knew it; expensive, white-walled, with pink shutters and an air of disdain, it stood in splendid seclusion at the far end of the beach.

'Oh yes?' I said politely.

'Wait! I haven't finished. The girl is Tracey Martin. Big sister is Annabel Martin. Remember her?'

'Of course!' I said, forgetting to be offhand. 'We saw her a few months ago in a T.V. play. What was it? *White Peacock, Black Swan*. And that comedy thing, soon afterwards: *There's A Lady At the Door*. I remember you *roared*... Annabel Martin – mmm!

What's she like, David?'

'As attractive as she looks on T.V.,' he told me. 'About thirty; blonde. There's something about her – maybe it's because she's an actress. Vitality, personality – oh, I don't know. And the cottage is a marvellous place – like something out of a brochure on "How to Furnish Your Home on a few Thousand Pounds"–!'

He fumbled in the pocket of his jacket, and tossed two tickets into my lap.

'Annabel Martin is doing a season of rep in the town,' he said.

'I know. I *do* read the local papers,' I said.

'Well, these are tickets for Saturday night,' he told me. 'The *best* seats! She insisted on giving them to me.'

'You two seem to have struck up quite a friendship!' I said.

I enjoyed the show immensely. Annabel Martin was not only a good actress, she was also, as David had said, a most attractive woman, with a vivid personality.

'She's *good!*' David remarked emphatically, as we drove home. 'Much too good for a little place like this – though she told me that she was doing the rep season just for the experience. She's rehearsing for a West End play, starting in October.'

Annabel Martin seemed to have talked quite a lot to David during his brief visit to Fisherman's Cottage, I reflected! I had a feeling that we hadn't heard the last of the Martin sisters.

I was right. I was preparing for surgery on Monday evening, when Annabel called – she was quite the most glamorous visitor ever to have called at Dr David Pembury's surgery! Slender, tanned, with vivid blue eyes, pale, silky hair, like her sister's, with the carelessly casual look about it that means it is expensively cared for. She wore a beautifully-cut blue linen trouser suit with a green silk scarf at the neck.

'Dr Pembury?' she asked, in her soft, lovely voice.

'He's out at the moment,' I said. 'I expect him back for evening surgery within the next half-hour. Can I take a message?'

I was about to add that I was Mrs Pembury, but I didn't get a chance – she looked at my white overall, consulted the small, thin platinum watch she wore on her wrist, and said:

'I can't wait, I'm afraid. Will you tell him I called, Nurse? My name is Annabel Martin.' She smiled as though used to creating an impression as much with the announcement of her name as with her striking good looks.

'I'm giving a party next Sunday evening,' she added. 'Tell him I'll expect him – around seven. You won't forget, will you? Thank you, Nurse!'

She was gone, leaving an echo of exclusive

perfume. Thank you, Nurse, indeed! I thought, outraged.

David came in about ten minutes after Annabel had left, and I gave him the message.

'A party?' he said approvingly. 'That would be nice!'

'I didn't know you cared that much for parties,' I replied.

'It will do us good to go out, Julie. We haven't been anywhere for *ages!*' he told me, reaching for the telephone.

I told him that Annabel had mistaken me for his surgery nurse.

'Quite natural,' he said. 'You should have introduced yourself, darling.'

I poured tea for us both. I heard Annabel answer the telephone call, listened to her delighted response when David said he would love to come on Sunday evening; and asked, casually, if he might bring his wife-cum-surgery-nurse.

'Oh!' I heard the small, disappointed monosyllable. 'Your wife? Of course! I didn't know you were married! So that was your *wife?*'

David hung up.

'All set for Sunday evening!' he said, with immense satisfaction. He looked at me. 'You're quiet, Julie – tired?'

'No,' I said, 'I'm not tired.'

I shopped carefully for a new dress to wear

Sunday. I knew exactly what I wanted – it had to be simple and look expensive. In the end I found a simple little sheath in tangerine linen. I had my hair cut and set, and bought a lipstick to match the dress. When I was dressed on Sunday evening, I asked David challengingly:

'Well?'

'You look very nice, darling; but then you always do,' he said.

Very nice! I thought irritably. That was the last thing I wanted; interesting, different, exciting – those were words I would much preferred to have heard from my husband!

In spite of my new frock, I felt like a sparrow amongst the humming-birds at Annabel's party; the big, expensively-furnished 'cottage' was full of good-looking men and attractive women dressed with clever, expensive casualness. Most of them wore trouser suits or such mini-mini-skirts that I felt middle-aged in my knee-length dress! They were all so poised, so very self-assured, and they all seemed to know one another...

Annabel greeted me charmingly. She was by far the most attractive woman there in a plain, dark dress that set off her good looks perfectly.

'I'd no idea you were David's wife!' she said lightly. Her tone of voice suggested I was much too ordinary to fill such a role,

188

her bright blue eyes gave me a quick head to toe inspection, and then returned to David. Her smile for him was warm and very friendly. *David?* I thought. People like Annabel Martin used christian names very easily, I reminded myself.

Tracey Martin came over to us.

'How is the foot?' I asked sympathetically.

'Oh, much better, thank you.' She smiled up at David, with some of her elder sister's charm in her tilted mouth and bright eyes. 'Wasn't I lucky that you were nearby!'

Clearly, Tracey thought that David was wonderful. This was just a teenage crush, I told myself, something any wife learns to cope with; and what on earth was the matter with me that I should wish the evening was over? Obviously David was thoroughly enjoying himself.

I did not enjoy my evening at Fisherman's Cottage. There was plenty to drink, an attractive cold buffet, people to talk to, and I should have been relaxed and easy. Maybe I would have been, but I saw how Annabel never moved far from David; and how adoringly Tracey looked at him.

The last arrival of the evening was a man called Stuart Taylor – tall, dark, immensely good-looking. I had watched him playing opposite Annabel in the play I had recently seen with David. When Annabel introduced us, I congratulated him on his performance.

He smiled down at me, and said:

'Thanks. It's always been one of my favourite parts. Being in rep learning a new part every week keeps one on one's toes.' He glanced thoughtfully towards Annabel, who was talking animatedly to David, with Tracey standing nearby.

'Your husband seems to have made quite a conquest, Mrs Pembury,' he said drily, and I had the feeling that he was displeased.

'Oh – doctors always seem very glamorous to people outside the profession; rather as actors and actresses do!' I said casually.

'Maybe.' He shrugged. His tone and look implied that Annabel and Tracey were enjoying David's company far too much. Well, I thought, with sudden pride, David could easily compete with Stuart Taylor when it comes to looks and personality!

After a few moments' conversation, he wandered over to the small group near the window; he said something to Tracey, who coloured and shook her head; and, as David came over to me, I watched him speak to Annabel. Just for a moment, her mouth tightened, and she looked furious.

I was glad when the evening came to an end, and we were driving home along by the sea-front, with a cool, salty breeze blowing through the open car window. David seemed preoccupied. I said teasingly:

'You've made quite a hit with the Martin

190

sisters, darling! Double conquest for you!'

'Don't be ridiculous, Julie!' he retorted sharply.

I was surprised; I had expected an equally light-hearted retort from him.

'Well, it must have been obvious to everyone,' I retorted. 'Tracey looking so adoringly at you, and Annabel being so—'

'For heaven's sake!' he cut sharply across my words. 'How you exaggerate, Julie! They were merely being pleasant! You sound as though you'd been watching me all the evening.'

'I certainly wasn't!' I retorted. 'I was teasing you, David! What's happened to your sense of humour?'

'Let's change the subject,' he said. 'I accepted the invitation to tonight's party because I thought you'd like an evening out. You're making me sound like the town's Don Juan!'

'You're the one who is being absurd!' I said coolly. 'I wasn't the only one who noticed, anyway. Stuart Taylor said you'd made quite a conquest, so it must have been obvious.'

'You sound like a nagging wife!' David said crossly, and spoke not another word all the way home.

Illogically, I turned my resentment towards the Martin sisters. Just the same, I couldn't help wondering why my teasing had so infuriated David; and then I realised he had been embarrassed, possibly because he had been well aware that Annabel was very attracted to him.

Our tiff was forgotten in next day's busy round of patients. I lunched with Louise Whittaker, an old friend of mine, and called on a couple of patients whom I had visited regularly during my district nursing days. Life was back to normal; last night seemed far away and unreal.

The following afternoon there was a telephone call from Annabel.

'Julie? Is David there?'

'No,' I said, 'I'm not expecting him back until five o'clock.'

'Ask him to call at the cottage,' she said. 'Tracey seems most unwell, and I would like him to have a look at her. Something she's eaten, perhaps. She's sick and complaining of pain...'

'Very well,' I said reluctantly. I had been on the point of asking her if tomorrow wouldn't do just as well, but I knew better. David, like all doctors, went when he was called, whether or not it was something that could have waited.

Anyway, it wouldn't really matter, I told myself; he would be back in time for our evening out – we had no surgery, and we had planed to drive along the coast to a favourite spot of ours, Sunset Bay. We had a table booked at the Sunset Bay Hotel, for seven o'clock. Plenty of time for David to go out to Fisherman's Cottage and back and get ready for our evening out.

It was just before five when he came in. I gave him the message. He downed a cup of tea swiftly, kissed me goodbye, and promised not to be long.

At quarter past six, I was ready for our evening date. It was a good twenty-minutes drive to Sunset Bay, and David would have to get changed, so he needed to hurry, I thought. He had been gone more than an hour, and it wasn't ten minutes' drive each way to Fisherman's Cottage. I was beginning to be uneasy...

I resisted the temptation to telephone the cottage. David was on duty, and a doctor's wife just doesn't do those things, I reminded myself; but whatever was wrong with Tracey Martin, it was certainly taking *time*, I reflected worriedly.

At ten minutes to seven I telephoned and cancelled our table. I telephoned the cottage and Tracey answered my call.

'David's just left,' she told me. 'There was something wrong with Annabel's car, and he's driven her to the theatre – she has to be on stage at eight o'clock. Me? Oh, I've got a touch of gastro-enteritis. Nothing much, really!'

'Nothing much! By the time David

arrived, I had reached boiling-point, and I exploded wrathfully when he came into the house.

'I've cancelled our table!' I told him furiously.

'Darling, I'm sorry! It was almost impossible to get away! Tracey seemed to want someone to talk to; that child isn't happy, and I don't know quite what's wrong. And Annabel insisted on my having some coffee and sandwiches.'

'All much more important than our evening out!' I flung at him. 'Annabel and Tracey Martin are just making excuses to see you, that's all! Tracey doesn't need a doctor. They're completely besotted, and you're thoroughly enjoying it! We don't have many evenings together, and this one was special, but it couldn't have mattered less to you!'

'Now, Julie, don't be ridiculous! I told you I couldn't help it–'

'Or didn't want to – because you found them so attractive, such amusing company. Well, you'd better go back and spend the evening with Tracey!'

Some small, inner voice told me I was being foolish and childish. I stormed upstairs, took off my best dress, put on an old pair of pants and a shirt and made a vigorous attack on the garden – *I* needed the exercise more than the garden did! David didn't come near me. At nine o'clock, I marched in with a tray of tea.

'I'm sorry,' I said miserably. 'But I *was* disappointed!'

'I know you were. So was I.' He put down the book he was reading. 'I couldn't just walk out on them, could I? And I was telling the truth when I said that I wasn't too happy about Tracey. You're an *idiot!* We'll go to Sunset Bay on Sunday evening...'

He held out a hand. Our quarrel had healed over, but I still felt vaguely uneasy. After all, David would have been less than human if he hadn't been flattered by the interest the Martin sisters showed in him. I was suspicious about the sudden fault in Annabel's car – especially when David began to tell me how interesting she was, how they had discussed her latest play on the way to the theatre, and how she had said she depended on him so *much...*

David said that he had told Annabel to telephone if she wanted him to visit the cottage again; and, sure enough, the call came a couple of days later.

'Julie! Ask David to look in,' she said, with the casual assurance of someone who knows she will always get what she asks for. 'It's Tracey – no, nothing very wrong. Just that she's a little under the weather, still!'

People much more 'under the weather' came to surgery instead of expecting a busy doctor to call, I told myself grimly.

Of course, David went to the cottage at once; he got back just in time for surgery; and two days later Annabel telephoned and said she wasn't sleeping well, and would David be a dear and look in...?

The morning after Annabel's last call, I met Stuart Taylor, as I was walking home to lunch along the promenade, after visiting Sally Allister. It was a glorious day, and walking was better than driving.

I almost walked into Stuart, and he recognised me at once.

'Dr Pembury's wife!' he said pleasantly. 'How are you?'

'Fine. And you?'

'I'm enjoying it here,' he said unexpectedly. 'Working in a seaside town in summertime has compensations. I rather fancy Annabel is very bored, though; and bored women get into mischief, Mrs Pembury.'

'What on earth do you mean?' I asked.

His voice was blunt, though his eyes were kind. He didn't mince words.

'Annabel is used to getting what she wants – and what she wants at this moment is your husband. He always seems to be at the cottage these days!'

I felt stunned. He added something about being forewarned being forearmed. He was in love with Annabel, obviously, which accounted for his anger at her behaviour.

He certainly *had* been angry when he had told me that Annabel wanted David.

I went home and told David what Stuart had said. I blurted it all out, never stopping to consider whether or not it was a wise thing to do, and I don't know what reaction I expected – but he was so coldly angry that I was reminded of the first day I had met him.

'You shouldn't listen to mischievous gossip, Julie. You've never liked Annabel Martin, and you've shown it quite clearly ever since that night at the party. As far as I'm concerned, she and her sister are my patients; I'm getting on with my job. Stuart Taylor would be better employed doing precisely the same thing!'

'I still feel you should ask another doctor to call on the Martins!' I insisted stubbornly.

'I've no intention of doing any such thing! Annabel is charming and friendly, and her sister is the same – no more. I shall continue to visit them when they need me.'

'Go ahead!' I retorted. 'Make a fool of yourself, David! You're flattered, you're thoroughly enjoying the situation...'

David never slammed doors; he just closed the door quietly and firmly behind him as he left the room. His refusal to send another doctor to Fisherman's Cottage only confirmed what I had suspected from the

197

beginning – that my husband was much more attracted to Annabel than he was prepared to admit, even to himself.

Miserably, I dressed for my afternoon with Miss Verney with whom I was going to discuss the final details of the Summer Fair.

Miss Verney had a problem, too! She said:

'I've been counting on Mrs Fairfield to open our Fair, as usual, Julie – and I've just discovered she and her husband will be on holiday, then. My fault; I should have made sure. But it would be rather nice to have a celebrity open it for us; I believe you and Dr Pembury know Annabel Martin quite well. Do you think she would agree? It would be *such* an attraction … *will* you ask her…?'

I closed my eyes, and thought how important it was that the Fair should be a success, because the money it brought in provided comforts for elderly patients at Christmas.

'Yes,' I promised, 'I'll ask her.'

Only Tracey was at home when I called, the following afternoon. She was sitting in a deck-chair reading, and jumped up eagerly when she saw me. I thought she looked pale and tired, and not very happy.

'Annabel is out,' she said, in response to my query. 'She's gone to the hairdresser's. But I'm sure she'll open your Fair for you, if you ask her.' She smiled, and it was a smile that gave her face a moment's maturity.

'Whatever people think of Annabel, she's a nice, generous person underneath,' Tracey added, unexpectedly. 'She has been very good to me. Our parents died when I was still at kindergarten and Annabel had a struggle to get where she is; but, ever since she's been earning a lot of money, she's given me everything I wanted.'

I pondered that remark, as I went home. I thought about David and myself, too, not feeling very proud of the way I had handled this present situation. I was always so ready to hand out good advice to others, so eager to tell them how they should deal with *their* problems. Well – I could apply a little of that good advice to myself. I had been tactless, suspicious – and behaved like a jealous wife. The fact that I *was* a jealous wife made no difference, I told myself wryly. I had handled a very ordinary situation very clumsily!

I went home, cooked David his favourite supper, chatted amiably about asking Annabel to open the Fair – and stamped down hard on my own feelings. David looked wary when I mentioned Annabel; but the real test came on the following Sunday, when Annabel phoned, and asked if David would look in during the evening, as she wanted to see him ... no, no one was ill, it was a personal matter.

I took the message to David, who was

busy gardening.

'But it's Sunday!' he objected.

'I know, darling,' I said gently. 'But if she's really bothered about something and wants to see you, then you ought to go, you know. I said you'd come this evening – I thought that was what you'd want me to do!'

'Sunday!' he said again, explosively. He threw down his trowel and went in to change. I sent him off with my blessing, and not *too* much concern that he should have been sent for on the one evening that he hated having disturbed!

When David returned – after an absence of more than an hour – he seemed pre-occupied; clearly, he had something on his mind; and, for the first time I could remember, during the time we had been married, he did not want to discuss it with me. I felt hurt, but I was determined not to show it; there's a time for waiting and saying nothing, I reminded myself – how many times have *you* said that to others, Julie Pembury?

Oh yes, I was learning a lot of things! I learnt another lesson, a few days later, when Tracey Martin unexpectedly called one afternoon: I discovered that one can size up people too quickly, and sum up situations wrongly, when emotions are involved.

Tracey brought me an enormous, expensive bunch of hothouse flowers.

'I think you deserve them,' she said, with charming candour. 'For all the times we've called your husband out.'

'A doctor – and his wife – both get used to that,' I said, rather awkwardly. 'But these are lovely – thank you! Will you stay and have tea?'

She accepted so quickly that I realised she was lonely. She told me that she was eighteen and had left school a few months previously. I suggested it must be boring for her, on her own most evenings, and with all her friends still in London – and then, as though floodgates had been opened, her story came tumbling out.

'I don't really mind; being here means I can be near Stuart, and that's what we both want. We're hoping to get married.'

'But I thought – I mean, I imagined your sister and Mr Taylor – were–' I stammered, lost my way and my words, and Tracey smiled.

'Oh no! He's eight years older than me, I know, nearer Annabel's age, but he and Annabel don't even *like* one another very much, though David has been talking to Annabel, trying to make her see how silly she is to make such a fuss about us wanting to get married. I may only be eighteen, but I *know* I'm always going to love Stuart, and no one else. In a way, I feel guilty, though, and sorry for Annabel. She's always been terribly ambitious for me, you see; wanted me to have the education she didn't have – and to become a doctor. I didn't mind that. I mean, I wasn't awfully ambitious to be *anything!*' she admitted, with disarming candour. 'And Annabel had set her heart on having a doctor in the family. So of course, when she knew about Stuart and myself, she was furious. She tells Stuart he isn't to come here, but he stands up to her and says there is nothing she can do to stop us. Still, it would be much nicer all round if Annabel wasn't so dead against it; we want to marry at Christmas. And David has been telling her that she's all wrong that she doesn't really care about me or else she'd want my happiness, not just the fulfilling of *her* ambitions – that was *his* phrase! She listens to him, anyway, which is *something...*'

When Tracey had gone, I sat down and waited for David. I had a lot to think about; I felt small and silly and ashamed – and the floodgates opened for me, just as they had done for Tracey, the moment David appeared. I told him all that Tracey had told me.

'I've been such a fool, David,' I ended miserably. 'I've been jealous – thinking you found Annabel Martin much more attractive than–'

'Than you?' He held out his arms. 'No, darling. All right, so I *did* find her remarkably attractive, and, like any man, I was flattered that *she* liked *me*. I'm human, you know, sweetheart!'

'And I didn't help – being jealous!' I admitted.

His arms held me tightly, reassuringly.

'Julie, I've been worried recently,' he told me frankly. 'Annabel is making no secret of the fact that she wants me. Even if I didn't have a professional reputation to think of, I happen to have a wife I'm very much in love with! Oh yes, Julie Pembury, you're an idiot, you have a shocking temper sometimes, you're jealous – not that I mind too much about that! – and all that adds up to love! Just the same, I'm handing the Martin family over to Dr Paice. Like you, I feel sorry for Tracey; but I've done all I can there. If Annabel won't listen to common sense, then Tracey and Stuart will just have to forfeit her blessing on their marriage. Annabel Martin is just storing up a great deal of unhappiness for herself, I'm afraid. I've never deliberately encouraged her, Julie. I don't like this situation at all – still, with Dr Paice taking over, that should be the end of it!'

That *should* have been the end of the affair; but I was troubled about Annabel, which sounds ridiculous, I suppose. Nevertheless, I visited her a few days later, to ask if she would open the Summer Fair.

She was alone, stretched out on a sun-lounger in the garden; she wore a white dress, the perfect background to her golden tan, and a pair of scarlet sandals. Looking at her, I think I could have forgiven David if he *had* surrendered to Annabel Martin's charms. She was the loveliest woman I had ever met.

'Well, hallo!' she drawled, pulling off her sunglasses, and looking at me with those shrewd, lovely blue eyes of hers. 'Sit down.' She waved towards a sun-chair, adding:

'And how's David?'

'Very busy,' I told her.

She lay back and smiled at me; she made me feel dull and provincial.

'I like David,' she said, with brutal frankness. 'Very, very much. He's handed me over to Dr Paice. I don't like Dr Paice at all; but perhaps it's just as well that David isn't my doctor any more – now I can entertain him here without worrying about what he calls his "professional reputation"!'

Her smile was knowledgeable, and I knew very well what she meant. Suddenly I felt sorry for her. She wanted David very badly and I knew he would never visit the cottage again.

Sometimes there is nothing one can do except be completely honest. I said to her:

'I love my husband. We've been married sixteen months, he works extremely hard, everyone in Ambersea likes him, and his happiness is the one thing I care about.'

'And what is all this supposed to mean?' she drawled.

'David is in love with me, too,' I replied gently.

'Really?' Her smile was cool and razor-edged. And then an odd thing happened; just for a moment, the glossy mask crumpled. Perhaps, as Tracey had said, Annabel was basically a nice person.

'All right!' she retorted. 'So I want David and I'm not going to get him – is that what you're saying? He's the kind of man women will always want – you may need to remember that, one day! A long, long time ago, I got engaged to a doctor, just out of medical school; he was very much like David. We were absolutely mad about one another – ah well, I was only eighteen! And then I was offered what's commonly called "a big chance". I took it. He said it was either marriage or a career – not both. *So* old-fashioned of him! I realised I wasn't the wife and mother type. My career is the most important thing in the world to me; I've never regretted my choice. You think I'm hard and selfish, don't you?'

'Not really. You've done a great deal for Tracey – she told me so; she feels such a sense of gratitude that she's unhappy about defying you to marry Stuart. But she's not cut out to be a career woman, and if you try to force her to be one, then you *are* being selfish – and foolish. Anyway, if you had really loved your doctor, your career wouldn't have mattered, would it? So you couldn't have been as much in love with him as you thought you were.'

'Words of wisdom!' she mocked softly; but, though the mask was back in place, her voice was not unkind.

'I'm not wise,' I told her. 'I make mistakes; like letting David see how much I minded that he came here to see you so often.'

'Oh, David lectured me about Tracey!' she retorted. 'All right, if Tracey wants to settle down at just eighteen and marry Stuart, she's welcome! I just hope she won't regret her choice. She'll be giving up so much. So you can tell David his treatment has been successful. By the way, Tracey mentioned that you wanted me to open a fête or something...'

I explained; she would refuse, of course, I thought. But she shrugged, smiled and said indolently:

'Yes, I'll open your precious fête! It will be something to do – I shall be glad to get out of this place, and back to town again!'

'Thank you,' I said awkwardly. 'For agreeing to open the Fair. And I hope the new play is a tremendous success.'

She put on her sunglasses again – perhaps

so that I couldn't see her eyes. Eyes are such a give-away.

'I'll see you at the fête!' she said, with an air of dismissal. 'Give my love to David. I won't be seeing him until then – if he's there; and I won't be seeing him afterwards. You needn't worry! What's that ridiculous old saw about hard work being the antidote to all ills...!'

Her mockery was directed against herself; I realised that, as I walked away. I remembered, thankfully, my happy marriage, and knew myself to be very lucky indeed – because though Annabel was a dedicated actress I believe she realised, underneath the price she had paid for that dedication; and I admired the courage with which she had accepted defeat over David.

All the same, I promised myself that next time David met someone like Annabel Martin, I'd behave *sensibly*...!

I almost ran from the cottage to the car. I felt as though I couldn't get home to him fast enough!

CHAPTER 9

It was a beautiful day; late summer, with warm blue skies, and a gentle breeze. I left the car at home, and walked through the park to keep my luncheon appointment with Nurse Barbara Connolly.

As I walked, I thought of all the things that had happened to me since the wild January day when I set out for the first time in my navy-blue uniform. District nursing is special, in that it takes one into other people's homes, involving one in the lives of patients as no other branch of nursing can; I had been eager and nervous; it had been a momentous day for me in many ways, for that first morning, I met David. I smiled over the memory – one of my most cherished. Just beyond the park, was the newly-opened Sombrero, and Barbara waited outside, looking remarkably pretty, I thought, in a cream linen suit.

'Julie! I've managed to book a window table – come on! The most gorgeous smells keep floating out, and I'm starving...!'

I had never known her so gay and full of nonsense. I should have guessed – but I didn't, until we sat down, and she nonchalantly eased the glove from her left hand to reveal a small, bright diamond on the third finger.

'You and Mother are the first two people to know!' she told me happily. 'Three guesses, Julie!'

'I don't think I need more than one. Malcolm?'

She nodded; her eyes were as bright as the diamond with sudden tears. Barbara had never been an emotional person, but I knew how deeply she had loved Malcolm Anderson, one of Ambersea's Probation Officers, for many months.

'I'm so glad for you!' I told her. 'I hope you'll be as happy as David and I have been – I can't wish you better than *that!*'

'I know! Malcolm is getting a lease on a flat early in the New Year, so we'll be married then...'

It was a happy celebration lunch. Not until it was almost over did Barbara say:

'Problem patients are your department, aren't they, Julie? I've got one – a Mrs Enid Privett. One of your nice friendly visits might help her. She's getting over a major operation, but needs more than my medical attention. Remember old Mrs Sinden...?'

I did indeed; I would never forget the poor old lady, neglected and unwanted by her daughter-in-law, over whom I had quarrelled with David, at our first meeting. I had insisted that something should be done for her, and he had pointed out that we could do no more than visit and give the kindness and attention her family did not give.

'Edna Privett is comfortably off,' Barbara told me, as though guessing my thoughts. 'She has her own house in Seagrove Crescent. Her daughter by her first marriage, Anne Ross, looks after her. Anne, thirty-five, teaches English at the local Grammar School and she has written a couple of children's books. Gave up her flat to come home and look after her mother, so Mrs Privett told me; she sounded as though she wished she *hadn't;* and the little I saw of Anne makes me think she's bitterly resentful about it. In fact, the place is simply charged with an atmosphere of the worst kind. I thought you might be able to do something; people *talk* to you...'

And I had more time to listen than had I been committed to a big daily round, as Barbara was; so I gathered up some magazines – my usual excuse for a visit – and called at Seagrove Crescent.

Enid Privett was a small, trim woman in her late fifties; not much in this house to compare with the worn linoleum in Mrs Sinden's room, the bitter chill, the shabbiness. Mrs Privett greeted me pleasantly.

'Nice of you to call, Mrs Pembury! I didn't know this was part of the district nurse service!' she said.

'An unofficial part! Anyone we think specially needs cheering up,' I told her cautiously; and, instantly, I felt her withdraw.

'I don't need cheering up!' she retorted sharply.

'Most people feel low, coming home after having been in hospital for an operation,' I told her. 'Home life is so different from hospital routine.'

'Oh, Anne is quite competent,' Enid said carelessly, and picked up a photograph from the table beside her – a pretty, fair-haired girl in her twenties, with a baby in her arms, and a boy of about four standing beside her. 'My younger daughter, Jacqueline,' she added proudly. 'I had a letter from her this morning, telling me she's expecting another baby – she and Harvey are hoping for a girl this time. They live just along the coast at Welbourne. Harvey works for a firm who manufacture plastics. He's just been made a director – at thirty-two!' The pride ran warmly in Enid's voice. 'He wouldn't have done it without Jackie to give him a push! She's a marvellous housekeeper, too, runs everything single-handed, except for a woman twice weekly!' She put the photograph back, and I said:

'Your elder daughter isn't married?'

'Anne?' The voice was a shade cooler. 'No.

Thirty-six next birthday and too independent. She got engaged six months ago; he taught at the same school. He broke it off, just before I went into hospital. Anne wouldn't say what went wrong. She's not like Jackie,' Enid added regretfully. 'Got a sharp tongue in her head; oh, she doesn't like looking after me, and she lets me know it! You'd think, being her mother, she'd *want* to ... Jackie's got such a sunny, good-tempered nature. Said *she'd* come and look after me if it wasn't for Harvey and the children. I'm going there for a holiday, as soon as I'm fit enough. Anne won't like that; she's always been jealous of Jackie. Jackie is the pretty one...'

'But Anne is clever,' I said slowly. 'I hear she has had two books published.'

'Oh yes,' Enid admitted. 'She's working on a third. Says they're as much to her as the children are to Jackie. Such nonsense! She should be married...'

'Marriage doesn't suit everyone,' I pointed out, remembering the disastrous mistake I had made in that connection about my friend Louise Whittaker.

'Well, lack of it seems to have soured Anne! She doesn't like looking after me – I can *feel* it. And if I praise Jackie she gets sarcastic and nasty!'

She went on talking about Jackie and Jackie's children with such obvious pride that I began to feel sympathy for Anne, even though she did seem to represent the disappointed old maid of popular fiction...

But I was wrong about that. I met Anne next time I visited Mrs Privett. It was a Saturday morning, and she answered my ring with a trowel in her hand, and wisps of grass clinging to the skirt she wore. For all that, she had a certain elegance, in her well-cut shirt blouse, her thick dark hair smoothed back from a clear-skinned face, with nice eyes and high cheekbones.

It was the eyes I noticed most; they were unhappy. When I explained who I was, she looked at the bunch of asters I had picked from our garden, and her smile flashed out briefly.

'Come in!' she said. 'I'm sure Mother will be pleased to see you. She's downstairs, sitting in a chair by the window. The sun seems to be doing her good. We're just going to have coffee; I'll put an extra cup on the tray...'

Enid looked pleased to see me.

'Hello, Mrs Pembury! This is my daughter Anne. She's allowed me to come downstairs today, though I'm quite sure she'd rather have me up in bed out of the way; but I've no desire to be a nuisance to anyone!' Enid said, with a faint air of martyrdom.

Anne flushed.

'Don't be silly, Mother!' she said shortly.

'I've never suggested you're a nuisance!'

'No, but you'd be getting on with your book if you didn't have to look after me; and you said this morning that your flat is much more labour-saving than this house.'

'So it is; just the same, I haven't complained!' Anne retorted crisply. 'You're at the convalescent stage of feeling sorry for yourself. You need someone to sit and hold your hand, and I'm not the person.'

'Oh, you never were very affectionate!' Enid said, with a sniff.

'Demonstrative, you mean.' Anne shook her head. 'I'm not made that way. People are different. We're not *all* like Jackie!'

Enid gave me a look that said clearly: There – what did I tell you?

'Too bad Jackie is tied down with a couple of youngsters,' Anne added. 'I'm sure she'd give more satisfaction as a nurse than I'm able to!'

Enid murmured something about people who lived alone getting selfish, and Anne whisked angrily out of the room. I didn't like the way these two sniped at one another – unnecessarily, and over the most trivial things, which made me sense some more deep-seated reason for resentment on both sides. Enid was tactless, Anne over-sensitive, unable to brush off her mother's remarks with good-humoured unconcern.

'I told you Anne didn't like looking after

me!' Enid said.

'I'm sure she doesn't mind...' I began; but Enid shook her head.

'She lets me know, in so many ways, how much she has given up. Jackie, now, would *want* to do it; so very different. Such a lovable person!'

'Perhaps Anne feels that you prefer Jacqueline, and this gives her an inferiority complex,' I suggested carefully; but Enid brushed that aside.

'Nonsense. Anne was always the same; she's always seemed to resent Jackie, since the time they were children. Well, she can have her precious flat back soon. As soon as I'm up and about again, I'm going to Jackie's for a month, and I won't need anyone when I come back.'

Anne had little to say, as we drank coffee together. I found conversation difficult, for she seemed reserved, as ready as her mother was with a sharp retort, and I felt for all the world as though I was sitting on a bed of thistles! I was glad to leave; as Anne showed me out, I said hesitantly:

'It think your mother feels guilty that you're trying to do two jobs – your own, and looking after her.'

Anne replied bitterly:

'She makes it difficult! I know she'd prefer Jackie, who has always been her favourite, and she never lets me forget it. Oh, I'm just

215

a failure to Mother!' Involuntarily, she glanced down at the empty third finger on her left hand. 'Jackie made a good marriage, she has an adoring husband, two lovely children. I can't compete with that! I was going to be married – then Keith met someone else... I saw her; she reminded me of Jackie!'

She sounded intensely weary. Was this the core of the antagonism between them? I wondered. Somehow, I felt there was much more behind it all than that, some reason that went a long way back.

I didn't mention it to David. He had enough problems of his own, poor darling, looking after most of Dr Paice's patients, as well as his own, while Dr Paice was on holiday.

A few days later I met Sally, in the park, proudly pushing the pram that held her baby son, William Allister. Marriage suited *her*, anyway, I thought – she looked so happy.

'Hello, Julie!' She sat on a park seat and patted the space beside her, looking like a schoolgirl in her gay cotton frock. I peeped in the pram at young William, chubby, contented and sleepy.

'*You* don't have any problems!' I told him, and Sally laughed.

'His mum does, Julie. How to stop his grandfather – *and* his father – from spoiling

216

him, for instance. Still, it's a nice problem, I suppose. Don't tell me you have any, Julie – you look much too carefree!'

'Oh, none of my own!' I told her.

'I know what that means! As usual, you have someone else's problem on your hands. Want to tell me about it?'

I was glad to talk it over with her; not that I thought Sally could throw much light on the situation between Anne and Enid, I reflected; but she looked thoughtful, and said slowly:

'Enid Privett – let me think, I know the name somewhere ... wait, I remember. Enid *Pine*. She went to school with Laura McCade. I remember Laura telling me once that Enid worked with her, for a time, at the Store,' Sally went on. 'Not that I was old enough to remember ... yes, I know! Laura was telling me that Enid was very good-looking and modelled clothes at afternoon tea, in the restaurant... Maybe she could tell you more about Enid.'

'Bless you, Sally,' I said gratefully; and she replied wickedly:

'Always glad to be of assistance, Nurse. Any other problem cases, just refer to me!'

I laughed, and admired William again, and we went our ways; I called in at the florist's where Laura worked, on my way home, and she remembered Enid very well, as soon as I mentioned her.

'We were at school together,' she confirmed. 'Good friends; I was sorry we lost
touch. Striking-looking girl she was; everyone expected her to marry well, and she had
to take up with a waster like Harry Ross.
Oh, he had plenty of charm, but I used to
tell Enid there was nothing to back it up.
She didn't listen – she was infatuated with
him. She had to get married to him, in the
end, and Anne arrived six months later. I
saw her sometimes, after that ... they
weren't happy. His charm had melted like
mist for her, and it was a loveless marriage.
He was always in debt, or out with other
women. Anne was a nice little thing, though
her father never took much notice of her.
She was just five when Harry died. It was a
release for Enid – he had treated her pretty
badly. A couple of years later, she met Bill
Privett and married him. They were
wonderfully happy – you never saw them
walking out together but they were hand-in-
hand, and Jacqueline arrived a year after
they were married. She was a pretty little
thing, not so reserved as Anne. Enid and
Bill had nearly twenty years together; I
reckon they were the happiest of Enid's life.
She missed him dreadfully when he died...'
I thought I was beginning to see daylight
at the end of a long, dark tunnel. That evening, I talked to David about my newest
'problem' family, while we sat over supper,

our precious 'end of the day meal' when we could eat leisurely, without fear of being disturbed.

'I think I understand,' I told David. 'Anne feels jealous of her half-sister – no wonder!'

David smiled quizzically at me.

'It's a very personal family problem, darling,' he pointed out gently. 'Tread carefully. Jealousy is one of the most dangerous of all emotions.'

'I wonder if Enid really cares more for Jackie because she was the daughter of a happy marriage?' I said.

'I shouldn't think so,' he demurred. 'Mother-love doesn't usually take account of those things, where children are concerned. I remember what a pretty little thing Jackie Privett was, though. And likeable. I attended her when she had measles and chicken-pox and all the other things children get...'

'Life's unfair!' I said angrily. 'People who aren't reserved are lucky twice over – first because they find relationships with other people easy, and secondly because people can *see* all their nice, attractive qualities. Reserved people have a far tougher time! People think they are stand-offish when they're just shy, and so they never take trouble to find out what they are really like underneath. I think Enid blames her eldest daughter for being *different,* and that's

219

wrong! Anne isn't the demonstrative type, and Enid should realise it!'

David sat back in his chair and looked at me thoughtfully through half-closed eyes that had a twinkle in them.

'You remind me of someone I used to know!' he said. 'Her name was Julie Barden and she was a district nurse; when I first met her she was in a fighting mood over an old lady who was being neglected, and she wanted to put things right. I'm afraid I threw cold water on her fire of indignation – rather unkind of me, I've since thought. I could have been more tactful. After all, there aren't many people, these days, prepared to do battle for others!'

I suddenly wanted to cry; there were times when I loved David so much that it was an ache deep inside me. I went across to him, put my arms around his neck, and my cheek against his.

'I was so worried about old Mrs Sinden!' I whispered.

'Darling, I know. I love you for it,' he told me. 'You've helped so many people, Julie, and sometimes, inevitably, you've been hurt. Go carefully this time, my love. Enid and Anne will resent having their deepest feelings exposed, even if you are trying to help!'

Usually I take David's advice, because it represents sound common sense. I *meant* to

220

have taken it this time...

In any case, there did not seem to be much point in my visiting Mrs Privett again. David was right, and there was nothing I could do. But though I hated not being able to help, I realised that the jealousies and resentment between Anne and her mother and sister went too far back, were too deep-rooted and complex for anyone like myself to sort out.

Unexpectedly, I saw Anne again, a week later; Lorraine Allison was entering some paintings for the Children's Hobbies and Handicrafts exhibition, being held in the Guildhall; the exhibition was held every year and this year it was intended to represent work the children had done during their long summer holidays.

Lorraine was a clever little artist. I admired her paintings, we put them in the back of the car, and drove to the Guildhall. The big hall inside was bustling with activity. I glimpsed Anne, helping half a dozen competitors to arrange a collection of seashells and dried seaweed, and I was surprised at the difference in her; she looked alive, absorbed in what she was doing, her hair ruffled, her manner carefree. Only when I went up to speak to her and saw her face clearly did I see the lines of strain, the bleakness far back in her eyes.

'How is your mother?' I asked her.

'Getting along very well,' she told me crisply. 'She plans to go and stay with Jacqueline in a week or so. I'm sure it will do her good.'

'I met a friend of your mother's, the other day,' I told her. 'Laura McCade. They went to school together.'

'Oh?' said Anne, her voice both sharp and cool. 'Then no doubt she filled in all the gaps for you!'

'I don't know what you mean!' I stammered, flustered.

The children had moved away. In our corner of the hall, we were isolated briefly, from the rest of the people working there. There was no one but me to hear Anne say bitterly:

'Oh, yes, you do know what I mean, Mrs Pembury! I've heard about you – you're one of those people who want to put the world right, sort out other people's problems, come up with an answer, and then file it neatly away under the heading: "Case closed".'

I swallowed my anger; I wasn't going to let Anne see how much she had hurt me. I merely said truthfully:

'I like people. Liking means helping, when it's needed; I haven't always known, until too late, when it *hasn't* been needed, and then I've only myself to blame if I'm snubbed. My husband calls it being impulsive; but he knows I'd rather make a mistake than not help someone who wanted kindness or advice. In your case, I've no intention of trespassing.'

Her answering voice was raw with an unhappiness that made me long to talk to her, even though I knew it was useless.

'I daresay you've been told that my mother had to get married to my father, and that he was no good! My mother hated him; she told me so, once.'

'But she loved *you,* the way any mother loves her child–' I began.

'You think so? No, I was just a reminder of that marriage, in the same way that Jacqueline reminds her of a happy marriage. Oh, she never made any distinction between us, so far as material things were concerned, when we were children! But I *know* my half-sister is her favourite. Apart from the father angle, Jackie had a head start – looks, personality, a successful marriage...'

'You're a success,' I pointed out. 'Jackie's pretty, I hear, but you have looks; and personality; plus an outsize chip on your shoulder that makes you feel sorry for yourself and spoils it all... I'm sure your mother thinks the same of you as of Jackie.'

'Then you're vastly mistaken, if you think that,' Anne retorted remotely. 'And thank you, I don't need your advice as to where I'm missing out on life. I think you should leave us alone...'

She walked away. I felt miserable and defeated, because I had wanted to help. David was sympathetic, when I told him about it that evening, but reminded me that the issues were too personal for any outsider to understand.

'Stop fretting about it, darling,' he told me, and eyed me critically. 'You're looking a bit under the weather. I don't know whether to prescribe a bottle of tonic or a sound lecture for getting yourself worried about what is happening to other people. Either way I don't suppose you'll take the doctor's prescription.'

'I know a better one,' I told him. 'Let's go out to dinner, David. There's no surgery tonight and I feel like having an evening out with my husband!'

It was a happy evening. Temporarily, I forgot about Enid and Anne. I looked at David, and thought: if I hated him, and had a daughter of his, would that hatred reach down and touch my relationship with our child? Somehow I was sure it wouldn't.

In the way that life has of turning up surprises, I saw Enid the following day. I was taking a short cut to see Miss Verney, driving along Seagrove Crescent. In the front garden of one of the houses, I saw a trim little grey-haired figure busily weeding.

I pulled up, and called through the open

car window:

'Well, you *do* look fit and energetic! How are you feeling?'

'Much better than when I was sitting around being waited on. Come in a moment, and I'll give you a bunch of those bronze chrysanthemums that you said you liked!'

I followed her through the house to the back, where she proudly pointed out the work she had done. Anne was kneeling at a border, busy with a trowel. She straightened when she saw me and gave me a cool 'good afternoon'. I couldn't imagine these two women gardening in harmony, I thought wryly.

In the kitchen, Enid tied up a generous bunch of flowers for me.

'I'm off to Jackie's next week,' she said happily.

'Judging by the way you're working now, you'll need a rest!' I told her.

'Nonsense! I enjoy gardening. Bill once said I had green fingers.'

'And Anne?' I asked. 'Does she have green fingers, too?'

'The roses are her province. She took a prize last year, at the Flower Show,' Enid said matter-of-factly.

'You must be very proud of her,' I murmured.

She looked at me sharply; no one ever

fooled Enid!

'What are you trying to say – out with it!' she demanded.

I hesitated, knowing I was going to blunder heavy-footed where I had no business to trespass and Enid added curtly:

'Anne said you'd met Laura McCade. All right, so everyone in Ambersea knew the story. It was a long time ago.'

'I don't think that part of the story matters,' I told her. 'I just felt that – oh, you and Anne don't seem to hit it off; and Anne's unhappy because she thinks she is a reminder of your first marriage, and that Jacqueline is special... She thinks you've always preferred Jackie. I'm sure she's wrong, but you talk about Jackie so much and make Anne feel she doesn't compare.'

I knew I had put it badly, and I didn't blame Enid for being furious.

'*Well!*' she cried, outraged. 'Of all the ridiculous nonsense!' She glared at Anne, who was coming in from the garden, brushing earth from her fingers, and said to her:

'What have you been saying to Mrs Pembury? That nobody loved you? Honestly, a woman of *your* age ... you were always jealous of Jackie, even as a child, but I didn't think you'd go to outsiders looking for sympathy you don't need!'

'I didn't discuss it with Mrs Pembury!'

Anne flared angrily at her mother. 'She chose to put forward her theory about why you and I have never really got on. I told her to mind her own business! But it *is* true – you've always preferred Jacqueline, always told people how wonderful she is; these last few years I've grown sick of hearing about her miracles as a housewife and a mother, and how she has helped Harvey to get where he is. You'd much rather have her company than mine; nothing I do for you counts in your eyes! Why don't you *live* with Jackie and her family?'

'Exactly what I intend to do! I've been invited to make my home with them!' Enid retorted. 'At least, I shan't feel I'm a nuisance there! You've made me feel I'm a burden, that you've had to give up everything to come and look after me!'

'I haven't–' Anne began; but Enid retorted:

'You never needed anyone; you were too self-sufficient, too independent. Jackie needs me. You can have your flat and your old way of life back again, soon enough!' She turned to me and thrust the flowers into my arms. 'You shouldn't meddle in what doesn't concern you, Mrs Pembury!' she added.

Anne glared at me.

'Exactly what I told you!' she snapped at me, still furious.

Well, at least they had agreed on one point! I escaped thankfully, feeling distinctly battered. They both blamed me for the quarrel, and I knew I deserved their censure; one day I would learn to keep a still tongue in my head! I reflected ruefully.

I thought that was the end of the affair, until I met Barbara Connolly, a couple of weeks later, and she asked me how I had got on with Mrs Privett. I told her the whole story, and she said:

'I have some news for you. Anne is at home, ill – suffering from nervous exhaustion. She's apparently been overdoing things, finishing her latest book and helping to run the Hobbies & Handicrafts Exhibition...'

I did not think a visit from me would be particularly welcome to Anne! But I felt great compassion for her; the broken engagement had probably been the last straw, and her mother hadn't understood that. On an impulse, I walked into the shop where Laura McCade worked, and asked her to send flowers to Anne. Laura handed me a card; I hesitated, not knowing what to put on it. Finally, I wrote: 'Sorry I meddled. Hope you'll soon be better. Julie Pembury.'

The telephone call came two days later; I thought it was from a patient, asking David to call, until I heard Enid's brisk, familiar voice.

'Mrs Pembury? Enid Privett here. Are you free this afternoon…? If so, perhaps you'd like to have tea with us…'

'Dare I?' I said ruefully; and, to my astonishment, Enid laughed.

'You'll be quite safe!' she said drily.

Nevertheless, I went to Seagrove Crescent feeling apprehensive as well as curious; but Enid greeted me very pleasantly, as though we had parted good friends at our last meeting, and told me:

'Anne is resting. Doctor's orders, she has to lie down every afternoon from two until four. She'll be down presently, to thank you for the flowers.'

'How is she?' I asked.

Enid, busy with the teapot, did not look at me.

'Much better for having had a rest. She ran the Hobbies & Handicrafts Exhibition Committee practically single-handed. Anne has tremendous organising ability which means people leave her to do all the work. And she never *would* admit to overdoing things; well, she has to rest now, and be looked after. She's like me, you know – much too independent.'

Like me! I looked at her in astonishment, as she handed across a cup of tea. And I realised she was thoroughly enjoying being able to look after Anne, who had always made it much too clear that she preferred to stand on her own two feet.

'Do parents ever really understand their children?' Enid suddenly asked me bluntly.

'Not always,' I said. 'Especially if the child is the reserved type, who finds it difficult to show affection or talk about feelings, and things that hurt.'

'You mean Anne, don't you? Don't look like that, I'm not going to accuse you of meddling again! I admit you gave me a shock that afternoon; so did Anne. She said some pretty hard things to me after you'd gone; but she made me *think*. I never *dreamed* her resentment against Jackie went deeper than the usual touchiness of an older sister for a pretty, younger one. I love Anne for her own sake – but *I* don't find it easy to talk about these things, either, though I'm going to have a shot at it when she's well enough to listen. Harry was no good, a waster – but Anne is different. Of course I'm proud of what she's done; her books, her job, the way she can organise. She never gave me a moment's anxiety, even as a youngster. Jackie did, sometimes, where the boys were concerned – I used to think she'd make my mistake with one of them. That's why I'm so thankful she made a good marriage. I tried to explain this to Anne, last night.'

I liked Enid Privett very much at that moment. She was an honest woman, and she was genuinely deeply fond of Anne, beginning at last to see that it was their similarity with one another that had caused such a tug-of-war between them.

'I suppose it was tactless of me to keep saying how wonderful Jackie was,' Enid added. 'It was a kind of retaliation, I think, because Anne always seemed to have a "down" on her... If Anne had talked to me years ago as she did last night, it would have been so much easier...'

I told her what I told David about the reserved people – who *needed* help and sympathy – finding life so much harder. Enid said nothing, but she nodded agreement, with a sigh.

'Does Anne mind very much, I wonder, that you'll be making your home with Jackie?' I asked.

Enid looked confused and embarrassed.

'As a matter of fact, Jackie *didn't* ask me to make my home with them – not that I'd really want to live with a married couple who have two lively youngsters and another baby on the way; but I was so furious with Anne...'

'Tell her that,' I urged; but I realised she did not know how to tell Anne the truth, for she was intensely proud.

'Anne is the brainy one of the family,' she added, with a half-smile. 'That was probably why I never understood her; I shall never forget the dumbfounded look on her face, when I told her so!'

By the time Anne came downstairs, I was feeling confident that it was going to be all right, after all. It wouldn't be *easy*, I knew, because people's characters do not change, basically; but, in learning to understand one another, they had taken the first step towards acceptance of each other, I thought.

It was a quarter to four when Anne appeared; Enid glanced up at the clock.

'You have no business to get up for another quarter of an hour!' she told Anne severely.

Anne opened her mouth to say something, then glanced at me, and saw that I was trying not to smile.

'I've had a good sleep,' she said meekly, 'and I thought, as we had company, I might be allowed down early.'

'I have to be strict with Anne,' Enid told me. 'Her favourite pastime is disobeying doctor's orders! She's too used to being the bossy one, and giving the orders – she told me last night she'd inherited her bossiness from *me!*'

Anne smiled good-humouredly, and thanked me for the flowers. She and her mother seemed awkward, for all the world like two strangers getting to know one another, but the atmosphere I had noticed on my previous visits was gone.

'Your mother will miss having you to look after, when you go back to school,' I told her.

'No; Mother will be busy getting things settled up before she goes to live with Jackie,' Anne said, with a momentary return to her old remoteness. She looked miserable and I asked Enid innocently:

'When are you planning to leave Ambersea?'

For a moment she glared at me, as she fidgeted with the hot water jug.

'I – er – I'm not sure,' she said. 'It depends; the baby is due quite soon...'

'Mind you, I should imagine you'll find it a lot less peaceful than being here,' I ventured. 'A visit, now – well, that would be different; but you said Jacqueline had asked you to stay permanently, I understand?'

'Well – not exactly.' Enid looked uncomfortable. 'A visit, yes; but after all, she has enough to cope with ... and *this* is my home. I don't want to give it up. Anyway, I can't stay with her at the moment; I've written and told her so. My place is here, until Anne is perfectly fit again!'

There was a silence. Would Anne construe that last remark as attention grudgingly given for a sense of duty? I wondered; but Anne rose beautifully to the occasion, her smile blissfully happy.

'Well, that's good news!' she said. 'Having given up the flat, I've discovered that it's quite pleasant living at home, and having a garden to look after. I'm glad I'm not going to be uprooted again!'

'Drink up your tea!' Enid told her daughter sharply. 'It's getting stone cold!'

I saw the rather shamefaced smile she gave her daughter, as Anne obediently drank her tea. I was so happy I couldn't wait to tell David the good news!

Then Enid added the perfect postscript to my afternoon.

'By the way,' she said, 'you'll never guess who delivered Anne's flowers. Laura! She called in on her way home, with apologies – it seems their van driver is ill, and she said it wasn't much out of her way ... she stayed for nearly an hour, and we had a long chat about old times. I'd forgotten half of the mischief we used to get up to at school! And it's been too long since we saw one another. She has invited me round to see her one evening next week. I told her I'd come if my patient could be trusted to look after herself for an hour!'

'Well,' said Anne demurely, 'if you're bothered about that, Mother, maybe Julie can come and keep me company!'

I said I would – I never gave a promise so joyously in all my life – and went home on winged feet to David, arriving ten minutes before surgery was due to open.

'Ha! I thought you were going to be late on duty!' he said, disappointed. 'Then I could threaten to fire you!'

'I wouldn't care! I'm much too happy. Wait until you hear...'

'I can guess.' He shook his head, with mock resignation before he kissed me. 'You've got another story with "Happy Ending" written underneath it!'

'Yes; it's my way of saying "thank you" for *our* happy ending!' I told him.

CHAPTER 10

Shirley Allison called, as I was tidying the waiting room, after evening surgery. David had been called out at the end of surgery, and I hoped that he wouldn't too late home.

'I've brought you a present, Nurse!' she announced happily.

I smiled. Lovable, red-haired Shirley would never call me anything but Nurse, in spite of the fact that my district nursing days were over.

'Something nice, I hope!' I said. 'I'm just going to make myself a cup of tea – like one?'

She nodded; we went into the big old-fashioned kitchen, and I unwrapped the parcel Shirley had brought me. Inside was a large slice of rich, iced cake.

'It was Lorraine's birthday yesterday,' she explained. 'I made this myself!'

'Thank you, Shirley. It looks *lovely* – I'll have it with my tea. Did she have a nice birthday?'

'Yes,' Shirley said; and while she talked, memory carried me back to the fifteen-year-old she had been when I first met her, looking after four younger brothers and sisters and her father. Her mother had gone away with another man and since then Shirley had managed cheerfully and uncomplainingly. I looked at the small diamond winking on the third finger of her left hand; she was engaged to a nice lad, Joe Soames.

'Joe is doing very well,' Shirley told me. 'He doesn't earn all that much yet, but it's *enough* ... we worked it out, and I've had a lot of experience of managing! We're going to get married in the autumn, Nurse. We thought October would be a good month!'

So *that* was the real reason for Shirley's visit! I looked at her bright eyes and excited face, and wished her happiness. I was delighted, listening to her breathless, happy plans. Shirley deserved all the happiness that marriage would bring her.

But there were bound to be problems, I knew.

'Who is going to look after the children?' I asked.

'Well, Sandy left school last month, at the end of the summer term. She's been looking for a job, and she thought she'd like to work in a shop. I *was* going to ask if you'd put in a word for her with Miss Carmichael – I mean Mrs Allister, of course! I told Sandy she needn't bother, now Joe and I have decided to get married quicker than we'd intended!'

'And how does Sandy feel about that?' I asked.

'Well, she didn't seem pleased. Funny. I mean, you're your own boss, in a way, if you're at home, aren't you? Still, she'll get used to the idea; I expect she's just nervous. Anyway, I'll only be across the road from her – that's another thing: Mrs Staples is going to rent us two rooms, and she's making her small room into a kitchen for us. Joe is going to help with the decorations – it's all worked out so nicely! And I'm getting a part-time job at the garage, to help out...'

Shirley was so happy that she bubbled like champagne into a glass. But – *Sandra?* I thought, uneasily. How did she really feel about taking over?

David came home in time for our evening meal, and I told him the story.

'I'd say Sandra isn't keen on taking over from Shirley,' he said. 'She's a different type; she probably wants to be out and about.'

'But, David, if there's no one else—' I began.

'If Sandra's heart isn't in the job, she won't make a success of it, my love,' David pointed out gently.

Sandra came, the following afternoon, to help me pack up the last of the toys for Miss Verney's Summer Fair. I thought she looked fed-up. Gently, I probed – and discovered, dismayed, that I was right. Sandra did not want to take over from Shirley.

'It's all right for Shirley,' she said resentfully. '*She* liked it!'

'I don't suppose she found it easy, at first,' I pointed out.

'Maybe she didn't, but she's keen on babies and cooking and things like that, and *I'm* not. I'd go dotty, in the house all day, with only Paul for company, and the other two kids coming home from school at four o'clock. I'd like to be out at work – the other girls at school, last term, were saying being at work would be a lot more fun than being at school. And I'd get a proper pay-packet every week, not just the housekeeping…'

Poor Sandra! I understood – and sympathised! Life beyond the schoolroom walls looked exciting, and she was eager to taste it. The prospect of cooking and shopping and baby-minding had no appeal for her, and she was honest enough to admit it.

As David said, when I told him:

238

'No two people are alike. Sandy won't feel the pull of domesticity until she falls in love – and that may be years away!'

'I have a feeling that this is only the beginning – that Shirley's wedding is going to bring a crop of problems,' I told him.

He took me in his arms, and said firmly:

'Just so long as you remember that *you* can't solve everyone's problems, darling. Though I'll admit you make quite a good job of those you do tackle. It would be a good idea if we had a family of our own for you to worry about! This house is big enough for a half a dozen, sweetheart!'

Sandra's reluctance to take over the Allison family was, as I suspected, only the beginning of the trouble; I felt so sorry that Shirley's happiness should be overshadowed by such things as the letter from her mother that she showed to me.

Shirley and Joe had put an announcement of the coming wedding in the local paper, and some 'kind friend' as Shirley put it scathingly, had cut out the announcement and sent it to Mrs Allison at Marlingham, where she lived with the man she had gone away with.

The letter was sugary with false sentiment. Beryl Allison wished her daughter happiness on two gushing pages, and then stated that she would be coming to the wedding.

'Dad is furious,' Shirley told me. 'He says

she *isn't* coming. I don't see how he can stop her.'

'Do *you* want her to come?' I asked.

'No, I don't!' She looked bleak and I knew that we were both remembering the occasion when Mrs Allison had promised to come home and had not done so; how eagerly Shirley had prepared for her, then, I remembered. Now Shirley was remembering, bitterly, her mother's fickleness and broken promises.

'I shall write and tell her I don't want her at my wedding,' Shirley told me baldly.

I would like to meet Mrs Allison, I thought; I'd like to see for myself what sort of person this shallow, butterfly creature really was... I was curious – and, unexpectedly, I had my wish!

I met her on the day of the Summer Fair. Shirley and Sandra came to help. Louise Whittaker whisked the three younger children, Lorraine, Heather and Paul, away to the beach for the day.

'I'll enjoy it,' she said briskly. 'I'm having them for the night, too, to give Shirley a break. It will do this old house of mine good to have a few children let loose in it!'

When we left the Fête, Shirley went off for an evening out with Joe, while I drove Sandra home. She opened the front door, and was just saying goodbye to me, when a woman came to the door. Sandra froze and looked at her with open hostility. Even without that look, I think I would have known that this was Beryl Allison.

She was small and plump and her hair had an artificial fairness, a gilded look about it, elaborately waved around her face. She was wearing a great deal of make-up that couldn't camouflage her age – she was in her mid-forties. She wore a too-tight sheath dress that didn't reach her knees. I saw the wink of stones on her fingers and at her wrists, and the heels of her glossy sandals were much too high for comfort and safety.

'Sandy!' she said dramatically. 'Where is everybody? I came home to see you and there's no one here…'

Her voice was high and petulant. I thought – wrongly, perhaps – that John Allison had been well rid of his wife. Sandra muttered something about going out again with a girl-friend in a few moments, and darted upstairs. Mrs Allison's eyes inspected me suspiciously, as though she thought I had kidnapped her entire family. I explained where everyone was, and added – from information Shirley had given me – that John Allison was working late.

'Well, it's really too bad!' she said. '*Do* come in!'

'I didn't want to go in; but David always says curiosity wins hands down where I am concerned!

Mrs Allison smelt of perfume, but it was the expensive kind. Her clothes were all wrong, but they were good clothes. Her man 'friend' certainly looked after her, I thought drily.

I introduced myself as Dr Pembury's wife and told Beryl Allison briefly how I had first met the family. I did not like her, and I did not want to stay, but I was curious to know what she intended to do.

She said, with a martyred air:

'Of course, you know my story. I went away with another man. Anyone can make a mistake – they don't get punished for it all their life.' Her eyes filled with tears, I imagined they came easily to her.

'I'm heartbroken that Shirley doesn't want to have me at her wedding!' she said. 'It's so cruel! I'm her *mother!* John has put her against me, hasn't he?'

'I'm sure he hasn't.' It wouldn't be of the slightest use to try and reason with her, I realised. 'He just feels that your being there would create an awkward situation, especially as everyone knows you went away with someone else,' I told her frankly.

'That's just it – I'm to be *pilloried!*' she said, with high drama in her voice. 'Shirley is my daughter – I want to see her again.'

'Once before you were going to come and see her,' I reminded her.

'I know. I was ill – and then Harry didn't

want to come. He doesn't want me to be at the wedding, and he's annoyed with me for coming here today.' She was very important suddenly, giving the impression that, for her, life was one long series of emotional crises.

'I told Harry I might come home for good!' she added. 'The kids are going to need me here with Shirley gone!'

I was appalled. Sandra did not want to take over, but I certainly wasn't going to play into Beryl Allison's hands by telling her so!

'Sandra is the same age now as Shirley was, when you left,' I pointed out. 'And very capable.'

'*I'm* their mother! My place is here! *No one* is going to keep me from my home and from my daughter's wedding. It will mean so much to me to see Shirley married.'

I wanted to laugh. I suppose it was wrong of me, knowing the issues involved, but Mrs Allison's excursions into drama were ludicrous.

At that moment Sandra raced down the stairs, and poked her head around the door.

'I'm going out!' she announced – to me, not to her mother.

'Sandy!' Mrs Allison said, outraged. 'Is that all you've got to say to me? Has your father turned you against me, too?'

'No! You never thought about us when you

went off – why do you want to come back now?' Sandra demanded; and she whirled out of the house, slamming the front door behind her.

I stood up.

'I must go. I have a husband coming home to his evening meal,' I said lightly; and I thought, with a moment's compassion, of John Allison coming back to find his wife installed in the house again.

Mrs Allison was furious with Sandra. She stood up and announced tearfully:

'This is my home and I'm not going to be turned out of it!'

'I'm sure you wouldn't want to embarrass Shirley and spoil her wedding-day,' I said shortly.

'Spoil it?' Beryl retorted, outraged. 'I have more right there than anyone else! I'm going to see my daughter married!'

Useless to tell her she had forfeited that right; instead, I let my simmering indignation boil over when I recounted the tale to David that evening.

He looked thoughtfully at me.

'Once you would have suggested it would have been a good thing if Beryl Allison came home, as Sandy doesn't want the job of looking after the family,' he pointed out.

'I've learned wisdom since those days, darling,' I told him. 'What on earth is going to happen? This is one problem that doesn't seem to have *any* kind of solution!'

He smiled and patted my head.

'Problems are like traffic jams. Ever been in a traffic jam, Julie? You know there's only one thing to do – sit it out; and, surprisingly quickly, everything will sort itself out. Wait and see!'

'I hope you're right!' I said doubtfully.

I went up to see John Allison the following evening. His wife had left the previous night, he told me, after a stormy session. He told me wearily: 'If she wants to come home, then, legally, there's nothing I can do. I shall hate it, and the children won't be happy; but I can't stop her from returning to her home, and she knows it. She always enjoyed being difficult...'

I met Shirley, a couple of mornings later, in the High Street. She was carrying a box with Carmichael's name on it, and I thought how miserable she looked.

'Hello!' I said gaily. 'Have you been shopping for the wedding?'

'Yes. My going-away outfit,' she replied, without enthusiasm. 'It's a tweed suit, quite a pretty green shade. Joe and I aren't having a proper honeymoon, because we can't afford it, but we're going down to Dorset for a few days, to stay with his grandmother.'

'You don't look very happy, Shirley,' I said.

'No,' she admitted dejectedly. 'Mum's

home. Arrived this morning – so I cleared out.'

Poor Shirley, I thought. The shadow of Beryl Allison would chill the bright warmth of her happiness; it was almost as though Beryl disliked the idea of Shirley, as the bride-to-be, being the centre of attraction, and wanted to steal the limelight.

'I think she's had another quarrel with *him!*' Shirley added.

I tucked a hand under her arm.

'Come and have a cup of coffee,' I suggested, 'and tell me what you'd like as a wedding present!'

I could see that there was something else bothering Shirley. Over coffee, she said:

'It seems as though Joe and I just aren't meant to get married!'

'Why not?' I asked.

'It's Sandy? Oh, I feel so mad with her! She doesn't want to stay at home and look after the kids, and says she's going to get a job! Of course, Mum has found out and she's *pleased* – says it's all the more reason why she should be at home, though if she thinks it's going to be easy to manage those kids, she's made a mistake. I never thought Sandy would let me down! I *had* to do the job, didn't I?'

There were tears in Shirley's eyes. I remembered her cheerfulness, her bubbling high spirits, her ready common sense, the endearing way she had of veering between child and adult when I had first met her. I longed to put my arms around her and comfort her.

'Sandy hasn't deliberately let you down,' I explained gently. 'No two people are alike, and she realises she will never settle down to looking after children and a home. You did a wonderful job, Shirley, but don't be angry with Sandy because she can't do it, too. If she was miserable – as she would be – then it wouldn't be a very happy home for your father and the children, would it?'

'No,' Shirley admitted. 'But what *are* we going to do – put up with having Mum around, knowing she could go off again any time it suited her, or just wonder who is going to see to things when I'm married?'

It was certainly the toughest problem I had ever encountered; I thought about David's 'traffic jam'. This one was going to be permanent, I told myself grimly.

I talked to Shirley about the coming wedding and some of the misery went from her face. Everyone, it seemed, was rallying around to make it a wonderful always-to-be-remembered day. She told me that Lorraine had been to the local hardware store and bought her an advance present – a tin-opener!

'I didn't know my cooking was *that* bad!' Shirley said, laughing.

'It isn't; but there'll be plenty of times when you'll be glad of a tin-opener!' I told her.

She seemed more cheerful when I left her; but I thought about her often, during the next couple of days. I could imagine that there would be tension in the Allison household, and I felt angry that Mrs Allison couldn't see how she was spoiling what should have been a happy time for the daughter she pretended to care so much about.

Sandy came down to the surgery a couple of days later.

'It's Paul, Nurse,' she said. 'He's got one of his chesty colds. Do you think Doctor Pembury would look, in, some time?'

'Of course,' I promised. 'Tell Paul he'll have to get better in time for the wedding!'

'I've got my bridesmaid's dress,' Sandy announced. 'It's pretty. Blue; and a little pearl cap on my hair. I'm getting ever so excited.'

'Is your mother still at home?' I asked.

Sandra pulled a face.

'Oh yes! It's awful, really, indoors. The kids don't take any notice of her, and you can't blame them. She keeps on to poor old Shirley all the time about no one wanting her because of what she's done, and how cruel we all are. Dad doesn't talk to her, but she nags at him all the time; and she won't do *anything* around the house; just sits there and smokes or reads or feels sorry for herself.' Sandra sighed. 'And Shirley is fed-up with me because I've got a job. I'm starting the week after the wedding. After all, if Mum's home, she'll just *have* to get on with things, won't she?'

David visited Paul; he expressed his opinion of Beryl Allison in no uncertain terms, to me, afterwards.

'She just hates coping, Julie. A sick child is a nuisance, a personal threat to her free-dom. It's Shirley who is looking after young Paul. Mrs Allison was full of complaints about the way she had been treated by her family.' He looked grim. 'She's a selfish, shallow creature, and two years of soft living have spoiled her completely.'

I fretted because I could do nothing; and then, as David had prophesied, everything sorted itself out.

I met Beryl Allison coming from a tea-shop in town; she was expensively and extravagantly dressed, she looked bored and petulant.

'How is Paul?' I asked.

'Oh, *he's* all right! Anyway, Shirley enjoys fussing over him!' she retorted. She looked at the car I had just parked by the kerb. 'If you're going my way, perhaps you'd give me a lift; the buses are all full this time of day,' she said.

Resignedly, I opened the car door. She complained, all the way, about the rudeness and disobedience of the children, her husband's coolness towards her, the un-pleasantness of the neighbours, how much she had to do in the house, and what a different sort of life it was from what she had been used to with Harry. I longed to ask her why on earth she had ever left Harry!

I said nothing; I just *simmered!* We reached the Allison house and she said self-pityingly:

'I never thought people could be so unkind. I'm not wanted here!'

I took a deep breath, and said all I had wanted to say to her for a long time.

'Yes, you *are* unwanted!' I said bluntly. 'Because you expect everyone to welcome you back with open arms, make life easy for you – while *you* do nothing. It's even too much trouble to look after your family, isn't it? All you do is feel sorry for yourself; try feeling sorry for the family you left without any thought three years ago! People will be frosty to you at the wedding – can you blame them? Your husband has had his life upset once, and now you calmly walk back into it again – can you blame *him* for not wanting you? The children are used to things as they are, with Shirley looking after them; you are almost a stranger to them, so naturally they don't take kindly to you. You didn't think of anyone except yourself when you left your home, so why expect other people to think of *you* now? You didn't consider them; you took what you wanted and now you have to settle the bill! You should have stayed with Harry, not come back to upset your family.'

'*Well!*' She glared at me, outraged and venomous. 'How dare you talk to me like that! It's none of your business. Who do you think you are? I suppose you've been talking to Shirley and making mischief? Of all the impudence...! Oh, I was a fool not to listen to Harry...'

She got out of the car, and gave the door a resounding slam. I drove home, blinking away tears. As soon as I saw David, getting ready for evening surgery, I ran into his arms and wept.

'Darling, what's this?' He looked concerned. 'Julie, you aren't well! It's not like you to cry ... what happened?'

'I've just done the cruellest thing I've ever done in my life!' I told him.

'Let's hear all about it.' He sat down in the big leather armchair behind the desk where his Uncle Daniel had once sat, and pulled me on to his lap. 'Come on, now...'

I told him, repeating word for word what I had said to Mrs Allison. When I had finished, he pulled out his handkerchief, wiped away the tears, and said firmly:

'Stop feeling so guilty, Julie. You told Mrs

Allison the truth. The truth is often cruel.'

I looked at him, astonished.

'And you don't think I meddled, David? That I should have kept quiet, because it was none of my business?'

'You meddled, maybe!' He smiled gently. 'Kept quiet? I don't know, my love. Someone needed to tell her a few home truths. And sometimes it takes more courage to tell the truth than to be kind and tell a lie. Remember that!'

I leant my head against his shoulder. David was such a comfort. He knew exactly what to say to restore my faith in life and people, but he never took the easy way out just to cheer me up. My spirits lifted. I wondered, should I tell him…? But no, not now, I thought. Anyway, I wasn't sure…

I learned from Shirley the next day that Mrs Allison had left. Shirley looked as though a cloud that had lain too long over the house had rolled away.

'She says she'll be back for the wedding, though!' Shirley said wryly. 'She went off in a huff. *He* called for her.'

I went up to see John Allison that evening. Shirley and Sandra were with him. I told him it was probably partly my fault that his wife had flounced away in a tantrum, and repeated what I had said to her.

He shook his head.

'She went because she was fed up with

being here and having to look after things,' he said. '*I* told her a few plain facts; don't you worry, Mrs Pembury.' He looked at Sandra, and added:

'The only argument in favour of Beryl being here was that the kids would have had someone. Not that she would have done much for them. *I* think it's Sandra's duty to stay at home, but she doesn't agree with me.'

'Things done from a sense of duty only aren't really worth having,' I said. 'Sandra's not like Shirley – she would only be miserable because her heart wouldn't be in the job...'

I explained to him, as I had explained to Shirley; I think he understood, but I realized ruefully that all the understanding in the world wouldn't solve his problem for him.

'There's no need to worry about the children,' Shirley said suddenly. 'I've worked it all out, Dad. I'll be living near enough to pop over and see the kids off to school in the mornings. Mrs Johnson at Number Six has offered to look after Paul during the day – you know how she likes having him, any time. I think she misses her own kids, now that the youngest has started school. Heather and Lorraine will have school diners, and Mrs Johnson says she'll bring Paul home at four o'clock, give them all their teas, and stay until Sandy comes

253

home. Then I'll come over in the evening, and put the kids to bed.'

'You'll never be able to cope with so much!' I told her. 'Looking after your own home, keeping a part-time job – and this! You *can't!*'

'Oh yes, I can!' Shirley retorted firmly. 'Joe is going to help. And Mrs Staples has offered to do a spot of baby-sitting. We've got good neighbours!' she told her father. 'They'll all help out.'

'There are school holidays,' I said. 'Miss Whittaker would love to have the children sometimes then. And if any of them are ill – oh, I know plenty of people who could help. It will be a communal effort – bringing up the Allisons!'

John Allison had never been a man of many words. He looked at his two elder daughters as though he was immensely proud of them and did not know how to say so; I think they understood. I felt proud of Shirley myself; trust her to come up with such a warm-hearted solution to the problem!

There was still the nagging possibility that Mrs Allison would return for Shirley's wedding, if only for the dramatic effect she would create; it was something we tried to forget.

Shirley made her dress, all by herself, and the traditional white satin gave her poise and dignity I had never seen before. Joe's sister was making the cake; Sandra never seemed to come down to earth at all, between the excitement of being bridesmaid and getting ready for her first job.

Summer gave way gracefully to early autumn, and the mornings had a crisp edge to them. Shirley's wedding day was only a couple of weeks away when Mrs Allison knocked at my door one sunny afternoon.

When I first saw her standing there, in a smart coat and a small, expensive-looking hat, I felt a kind of weary resignation; well, we couldn't expect *everything* to be perfect, I reminded myself.

I looked past her at the big cream car pulled up at the kerb. A man was seated behind the wheel, plump, florid, expensively dressed.

'I've just been to collect the rest of my things,' she told me aloofly. 'There's no one at home, so I thought *you* might give Shirley a message, as you're so friendly with her.' She made a small sneer of the word 'friendly'.

She smoothed on her expensive gloves, and I saw the flash of a gold charm bracelet at her wrist.

'Harry and I are going abroad for a holiday,' she added, with elaborate casualness. 'Harry made a nice little sum on a business deal, and he says we may as well enjoy it. We're going right away, so I won't be here for the wedding. We'll probably go to Paris.'

My spirits soared. I wondered as to Harry's morals, businesswise, but it was nothing to do with me! And I suspected that taking Beryl Allison away was a manoeuvre on his part – he was probably feeling worried about her renewed interest in her family.

'At least *he* wants me,' Beryl Allison told me spitefully. 'I must have been mad to have come back here. Why, Harry makes more in a day than John does in a month! And he likes spending it – on me. I'm not going to be tied down with kids again, and spend my days doing housework and cooking! I'm going to enjoy life. Harry knows how to look after me. You can give Shirley my best wishes, and tell her I'll send her a decent present...!'

With that, she flounced away, and got into Harry's car, probably hoping I was impressed. It was the last time I ever saw her.

I had an appointment that afternoon. Afterwards, I called on Shirley. It was a lovely day; the leaves came down in a golden snowstorm, the sun was warm and kind, and I wanted to dance along the streets for sheer joy of living. I had never felt so happy – not even on my wedding day.

I told Shirley her mother had called on me.

'She was very sorry to have to miss the wedding,' I said, 'but she felt it was the best thing, after all, rather than embarrass you and spoil your big day. She won't be back Shirley – not for good; but she sent you her good wishes for a lovely day and she's going to send you a present. She feels the right thing for her to do now is to make her life with Harry.'

'I hope she'll be happy,' Shirley said soberly. 'As happy as I'm going to be with Joe. I love him so much, Nurse. I want things to go right for us; maybe Mum wishes sometimes she hadn't gone off, like that. Still ... oh, everything is going to be all right now!'

I echoed Shirley's sentiments as I went home. She looked as happy, as carefree, as any bride-to-be had a right to look, and I wished her all the joy in the world, for she had courage, humour, common sense – and a big heart.

David was home early for tea; it was warm enough for me to open all the windows. I put out the best china and the silver tea-service, feeling it was an occasion that merited them, and wondering if he would ask *why* ... but he didn't notice them!

I told him about Mrs Allison's visit, and repeated what I had said to Shirley.

'Bending the truth again, eh, Julie?' he said wickedly. 'All right, darling. I know why you did it – so that she should have a pleasant memory of her mother. I think it was a nice thing to do. Julie, you look different today – like a cat that's swallowed the cream. What have you been doing?'

My heart was turning somersaults, but I managed to answer him casually. I sat back in the chair, looking at the garden afire with chrysanthemums and michaelmas daisies. The house seemed to hold me warmly and contentedly, a safe place for David and myself and our children.

'Doing?' I said casually. 'Why, nothing, darling. Only planning my wedding outfit. I've got the dress – it's just the accessories. It's a pretty dress, David – pink. You like that colour; and these new, loose dresses are awfully good at keeping secrets. Not that I think anyone will guess – it's too soon. I kept a special appointment this afternoon, David – though I already *knew!* It will be an early spring baby – in time for our wedding anniversary. Are you pleased? *I'm* so thrilled!'

It took him several seconds to really take it in; then he was out of his chair in one stride, almost overturning it. His teacup crashed to the floor and lay there, shattered into small pieces – I didn't even care that it was one of the best ones – not with *that* kind of look on my beloved David's face!

'Oh, *darling!*' He held me so close that I

could scarcely breathe. 'That's *wonderful.* Am I pleased, indeed? What do *you* think, Mrs Pembury? Now you'll *have* to resign as surgery nurse, and you'll be too busy bringing up our family to worry about other people's problems!'

'I don't think I could be too busy for *that!*' I murmured.

'I'm selfish. I hate sharing you with all the world. You'll always try to put the world right, Julie, and I'll always love you for it. A *baby!* I don't care whether it's a boy or a girl!'

'Maybe triplets!' I whispered mischievously. 'You once said we'd have triplets and surprise everyone!'

His laughter, carefree and exultant, filled the quiet room. I thought of my first day at Ambersea, a new and rather scared district nurse in a brand-new uniform. That was the day I had met David. I hadn't known, then, just how much happiness life could hold.

'I love you,' he whispered.

'I love you, too. David; and, by the way, I'm still your surgery nurse, until you get a replacement. Time I was putting on my overall. And I have your surgery to prepare, Dr Pembury! This is your busy evening!'

Laughing, hand-in-hand, we went out of the room together.

CHAPTER 11

When I married David I thought life could not hold any more happiness for me; and I was wrong. The joy I had known, working in Ambersea, getting to know David, whom I had so fiercely hated at our first meeting, finally realising that we loved one another, and the sheer bliss of nearly two years of marriage was nothing compared to the delight of knowing our first baby was due at the end of March.

That Christmas was such a happy one. My parents came to stay. So did Clare Martin, my friend from hospital training days, now a district nurse herself. Time was when I had tried to pair Clare off with Alan Roberts, an old flame of mine! Clare laughed about that.

'Alan and I are good friends, no more! We meet sometimes, when I get up to town, which isn't so often these days. I'm happy as I am, district nursing. Mind you, there's a charming doctor at the local hospital, and we seem to keep bumping into one another...!'

A happy Christmas; a gift from the Gods, perhaps, made with compassion. The coming year looked as enchanting as the lights on the tree, and we toasted it joyfully.

January was a bland month, deceptively mild and gentle. I was no longer able to act as surgery nurse to David, and he had a new one, Marilyn Adams, young, pretty and capable.

Early in January I went to the wedding of Barbara Connolly, a district nurse friend of mine. Ruefully, I told Sally Allister:

'Modern maternity clothes are wonderful, but at this stage even *they* can't do a great deal for a very pregnant mum-to-be. I feel large and weighty!'

'You are too!' Sally said wickedly. 'Never mind, honey!' she added, laughing. 'I'll be looking large and weighty again myself, at the end of the summer!'

I blinked at her in astonishment, and she nodded.

'There'll be an addition to the family in August. Doug is thrilled, so is Father. There'll only be sixteen months' age difference between William and his brother or sister, but I think that's rather nice; they'll be good companions, much more than with a gap of four years or so between them!'

'Sally, that's wonderful news!' I told her.

'I'm glad you think so!' she said drily. 'I told Mrs Hobson, when she came to clean this morning, and she looked shocked, as though there was something slightly indecent about having another baby so soon. "Only sixteen months," she said. "Only sixteen months, Mrs Allister. Well, well."!'

We laughed together about Mrs Hobson, whose four children had all been born at neatly spaced three-year intervals.

Sally and Doug were making great plans for the future. She used to meet me in the park afternoons and let me push young William – good practice for me, as she said! – before coming back to tea by the fire. I thoroughly enjoyed those afternoons, and my long talks with Sally. She had her problems, too, although they were only fist-sized clouds, in a summer sky.

'Doug is having a new house built for us, outside the town,' she said. 'We chose the site and bought the land before Christmas. He says country and sea air is better than town air for children. I agree with him, and we'll only be half a dozen miles from Father; but I know how much he's going to miss us, living alone again in that great house of his. He says there's plenty of room for half a dozen children to grow up in the place. That's true, but we need a home of our own.'

I agreed with her, though I felt sorry for Mr Carmichael. He was in his late fifties, and Sally was his only child; her mother had died soon after she was born, and, until Sally was expecting William, she had worked at the store with him. I knew how much he missed her there as well.

'Couldn't you persuade him to buy a smaller house, near where you and Doug are planning to live?' I asked.

She shook her head.

'He'll never leave the House on the Hill. I wish he would. Seems all wrong he should be alone there with only the housekeeper, and Mrs Hobson coming in every day. He doesn't need all that space; but the house is full of memories for him. He should have had a dozen sons, not one daughter!'

I smiled down at William.

'There's his grandson,' I reminded her. 'Maybe two, this time next year.'

'Oh, I know! He loves to have me tell him that! Sometimes I *have* thought that it would be nice to go on living at the House on the Hill, with the children growing up there, and me going back to work for Father when they're old enough; but that isn't fair to Doug.'

And Sally loved her ambitious young husband too much to deprive him of the right to create his own home for his wife and family, I thought; just the same, I knew it wouldn't be easy for her to leave her old home, when the time came. Mr Carmichael had given them the top floor as a flat for themselves. Still, it *wasn't* the same, to Doug, at any rate, I reminded myself; and

David agreed with me.

'Doug gets on very well with his father-in-law,' David told me. 'But he has his own way to make. I believe he is doing very well indeed. I saw Louise this morning, and she went into raptures over some new kitchen furniture display in Carmichael's window – "designed by Douglas Allister". She told me to tell you it's ruinously expensive, but she *must* have it, and you and I are to go and see it when it's installed in her kitchen!'

This we did. Louise had, to use her own words 'gone mad over her kitchen'! The furniture, white-painted, had an unusual design cut out of the wood in the high-backed chairs, and both chairs and the round table were painted with a design of ivy leaves and forget-me-nots.

'Isn't it beautiful?' she said dreamily.

'Is it true,' David asked solemnly, winking at me, 'that no one is to be allowed to use it? That it's only to look at...?'

We laughed; and Louise made us coffee. I felt contented, lapped in a warm sea of happiness.

After gentle January, February was a loud-voiced, angry month, stamping in with snow flurries, and bitter winds with destructive fingers that pulled slates from housetops and branches from trees; after the winds came the rain, dismal, as persistent as the round of coughs and colds that kept David so busy; and the fogs. Thick yellow fog was almost unknown in Ambersea – this was a sad sea-mist that hid the beach and the sulky seas from us.

It wasn't weather for walking in the park, so Sally often dumped William in her small car, and came to see me.

Her father still drove himself to the Store every morning in the large, sedate black saloon that had been his pride and joy for ten years and used an enormous amount of petrol; but it was a very distinctive car, and everyone in the town recognised it, so that he smiled tolerantly when Sally teased him about his 'museum piece.'

I still remember, vividly, the February afternoon that Sally came to see me, six weeks before my baby was due. It was a cold grey day, the streets misted with rain, the sea-fog making the afternoon seem shorter – and cosier, as we played with William in front of the big fire, and made toast for tea. There were expensive, out-of-season flowers that David had bought me, standing in a jug of smoky grey glass, a hint of spring to come and promises fulfilled; outside, the world could be as colourless as it pleased – in here, all was peace and laughter.

'Babies are fun,' Sally told me. 'Especially at this age, when you have a perfect excuse for wasting time playing with them. Heavens, look at the time – nearly half past four! Doug has driven up to London – one of the big stores is interested in his designs! I'm thrilled to bits – it could mean a marvellous contract; he said he'd be back early this evening, and I must be there to hear his news...'

She began to gather up William's toys – the miniature teddy-bear that Mrs Dellar had knitted for him, the mournful-looking panda, the plastic cube that had entranced him with its flurry of snowflakes tumbling over the little house inside, when the cube was shaken.

'So Doug has driven up?' I said. 'Are you forgiven for denting his bumper and making a mess of his headlamp...?'

She laughed.

'Yes! He was furious with me – for ten minutes! Said I'd turned in at the gates of the House on the Hill often enough to know how to miss them, instead of taking a lump out of the post at the side. Said he'd never have let me drive his car if he had known – but I told him, I'm used to smaller cars than his tycoon affair! Anyway, he took me out to dinner just to prove he wasn't thinking of divorcing me, and Father dropped him off at the garage this morning to collect the car ... he said if the car wasn't ready he'd go up to town by train; but the garage won't let him down!'

She scooped up William and held him

close to her, laughing, happy, her expensive fur coat slipping back from her shoulders, the firelight gleaming on her soft, pale hair. I thought she had never looked so pretty. I went to the door, and waved her out of sight, as she drove away with her son. A girl would be nice for them, next time, I thought. Sally and Doug would have lots of children, and enjoy them all. Sally had been a lonely child, in spite of boarding school, and Doug had only an older, married sister, living abroad.

I knew David had a heavy round, and would be late that night, with only time to swallow a quick cup of tea before surgery began. I was gathering the used tea-things together when I heard a knock at the door.

It was Shirley Soames. She looked radiantly happy, muffled to the eyebrows, and she thrust a parcel into my hand, shaking her head when I invited her in.

'Can't stop, honestly, Mrs Pembury, though I'd love to … I like to have Joe's tea ready when he gets in, and then I pop over and see to the kids … this is a present for the new baby. Come and pay us a visit soon!'

When she had gone, I opened the parcel. Knitting was amongst Shirley's many talents, and the pram set she had made for me was so exquisitely knitted that my eyes filled with tears.

David barely had time to swallow his cup of tea, before surgery. I switched on the television for the news, only just in time – for the announcer was saying that there had been a train crash ... and when he announced where it had occurred, I sat upright, for it was this side of the Junction, less than twenty miles from Ambersea. The impersonal voice said that the train had been due at Ambersea at a quarter to six ... there were several people injured, some seriously, and some killed ... final details were not yet available...

I was appalled. People going up to town for a day's shopping come back on that train, because it was a good, fast one. David and I knew so many people in the town that I was uneasy, wondering if anyone we knew had been there.

When David came in from surgery, I told him at once about the accident ... we listened to the news just before nine o'clock. Ten people had been killed and thirty injured.

'A nasty business,' David said grimly. 'The fog was thick in town today, I heard... I suppose we won't get any names until the morning papers. You look tired, darling; I'll make us some coffee.'

I dozed in the firelight, thinking rather unhappily about the train disaster and the sadness it would bring to a good many homes. The telephone began to ring as David set the tray beside me, and, resignedly, he went to answer it.

He seemed to have been gone a long time; when he came back his face was drawn and unhappy, his eyes looked bleak.

'What is it, David?' I asked fearfully.

'Darling.' He came over and put his hands on my shoulders; his voice was very gentle. 'I have something to tell you – try not to be too upset, Julie. Someone we know was killed in the train disaster...'

'Who was it?' I whispered; and in the split second before he spoke, I guessed...

'Douglas,' he said briefly. 'He was alone in a first-class compartment at the front of the train. He was killed outright by the crash. That was Mr Carmichael, on the phone; Sally insisted on going to the Junction with him, when they got the news. He's just brought her back, and he's asked me to go up to the house right away...'

I put my hands over my face. I felt cold and sick and terribly shocked. I began to shiver violently, and as David handed me my coffee, I wept, remembering Sally with William in her arms, laughing, only hours ago.

'Let me come with you!' I said.

'No.' His voice was firm. 'It won't do you any good, and I have you to think of, you know, darling ... besides, Sally is shocked and hysterical and needs something to make her sleep. You can see her tomorrow.'

I knew he was right. He kissed me and went out into the night, and I sat there, hardly able to hold the cup because my icy hands were shaking so much. After the first numbness, I felt incredulous horror, and then a terrible, tearing pity for Sally, who had possessed everything, and now had nothing. *If the car wasn't ready ... if the car wasn't ready* ... the words jogged in my mind, like silly, twisting puppets, jerking on strings, performing the same movements, over and over again...

It was more than an hour before David returned. I was quite calm then, impatient to hear what he had to say.

'She's asleep,' he said briefly. 'It wasn't easy ... she was in a dreadful state, naturally. I offered to bring William back here, but Mr Carmichael wouldn't hear of it.'

'Will she lose the other baby?' I asked fearfully.

'Not if we can help it. There is a danger, though.' He sighed, running his hand through his hair. 'Poor Sally! All I could do was to see that she slept for a few hours; she'll wake up, and remember, and she'll keep on doing that for a long, long time, until she begins to recover. Don't look so unhappy, darling. She *will* get over this, and remake her life again, because people do –

it's the time in between that drags so heavily it hurts.'

I leant against him, and whispered:

'I won't know what to say to her, David. That serves me right. All this time I've prided myself on knowing exactly what to say to people, how to solve their problems, how to make their world right ... so much good advice, so many silly words, all the trite little phrases that don't help; and when something like this happens, I haven't any *real* words to say!'

I slept badly that night. David knew. He held my hand and said nothing at all, but his silent closeness was all the comfort I needed. I knew he was worried about *our* baby, due in six weeks' time.

There were photographs and reports of the accident on the front page of the morning paper. Amongst the 'slightly injured' was June Whitton, and I remembered the day she had first come to the surgery. One of Dr Paice's patients had been seriously injured; I knew no one else – except Douglas, about whom there was a short paragraph.

David drove me up to the House on the Hill that morning. It was raining, and the roads were greasy. The trees around the big house seemed to huddle together. Mrs Hobson, who let me in, had been crying. Mrs Greaves, the housekeeper, had William in her arms, and he chuckled and thrust a fist at me. I tried not to cry as I walked up to the big room on the first floor where Sally lay against the pillows of a double bed, her face without any colour, her eyes bright and hard. She never moved, when I came and sat down beside her, just looked at me as though she was seeing me through the wrong end of a telescope. I thought: *I wish she would cry...*

'Hello, Julie!' she said, in a high, bright voice. 'I think they're going to take me to hospital, because they're afraid I may lose this baby. It doesn't matter! I don't want the baby, anyway. It's my fault that Doug was killed. Father says that's nonsense, but it's true, isn't it, Julie? If I hadn't damaged the car, he would have driven up to London; but the car wasn't ready and he had to go on the train. I offered him my car, but he said no, I needed it for shopping, and anyway his was *sure* to be ready, the garage never let him down. So I killed him...'

I let her talk. I let the tide of that bright voice flow over me, because there was nothing else I could do. I felt emotionally bruised and battered, and, deep inside, there was a terrible sense of failure because I couldn't help Sally, when she needed help so badly.

'...Father said no one was to blame. Or perhaps the garage, because they *had* let him down. One of the mechanics drove round to pick up Doug on the quarter to six … Doug asked him to … but, you see, it was my fault the car was in the garage, Julie … I shall always have to remember that, won't I, that I was guilty…! He would be here, now, but for me … because I was careless…!'

Poor Sally. I wept for her, and she looked surprised. She had to go on telling herself over and over again that she was guilty, fixing her mind on that one fact, because she did not dare to think about the other, terrible things, like Douglas never coming back to her again.

'Sally,' I said gently, 'don't blame yourself. Doug wouldn't want you to do that. Remember the two happy years you had. You've got William as a reminder of them, and another baby…'

All the trite little things! a voice inside me mocked. Sally looked at me, a cold, angry look, and said remotely:

'What do you *know* of unhappiness, Julie? Nothing at all – any more than I did, this time yesterday. Oh yes, you can talk to people, and help them, and make things right for them – but this is one thing you can never make right… You don't understand. Why don't you tell me that I had two happy years and some people don't have that much? Some people have much, *much* more than that!… How will you answer that?'

273

She turned her face from me, looking out of the window at the bare tree branches against the grey sky, the sprawling town below, half-hidden in thick mist.

Back home, I sat and wept, until David was worried and angry.

'Julie, stop it! There *are* some things you can never put right, and only time will soften the sharp edges for Sally. You've got a sense of guilt, too, because you can't find an easy remedy for Sally's misery, one that she's going to accept meekly. You've got a husband to think about – and a baby almost due. Have you forgotten that?'

David was concerned that Sally would lose *her* baby, and he insisted on her remaining in bed – a fact which she accepted with bad grace and the stubborn insistence that she couldn't care less about the coming baby. I went to see her again, but her mood was one of bitterness, and I could not reach her. I knew David was also worried, because, after her first shocked hysteria, Sally had shed no tears. He was afraid if she did not bend to her grief, she would snap like a brittle twig.

I think I shed enough tears for us both. How do you help someone who knows the greatest sorrow of them all? I thought. Perhaps I should accept what David told me so often – that the only help one can give is thought, loving sympathy, understanding...

It was a few days after the accident that Miss Verney invited me to tea. I did not want to go, but David insisted that it would do me good, as I had not been out of the house for days, except to see Sally. I decided to walk; it was an unexpectedly good day, the rain and mist having given way to gentle sunshine, and I had a sudden burst of physical energy. I needed both the exercise and the fresh air, I thought.

When I was leaving the house, I remembered guiltily that I had not thanked Shirley for the beautifully knitted pram set she had given me. Subsequent events had completely driven the thought from my mind, so I made a detour that took me to the bright little house, just across the road from her old home, where Shirley and Joe had two rooms.

She was delighted to see me, and showed me her small flat with pride. It looked cheerful, clean and gay, and she glowed with pride when I congratulated her.

'Marriage suits you, Shirley,' I told her.

She nodded blissfully.

'So everyone says! Oh, I'm so lucky, Mrs Pembury – Joe is wonderful!' And then, for a moment, she looked thoughtful, a shadow of concern crossing her bright face, as she added:

'Isn't it dreadful about poor Mrs Allister? Joe was saying last night, if only he'd gone in the car ... that sort of thing makes you think, doesn't it? It was in the garage where Joe is ... he was working on it...'

I remembered, then, that Shirley worked in the office at the same garage as Joe. I hadn't realised, until this moment, that it was the garage Douglas Allister used.

I said slowly:

'Mrs Allister is blaming herself, Shirley – because she damaged the car, and it had to go in for repair.'

'Oh, it would have been in the garage anyway, then,' Shirley replied. 'On the day he bought it in to be repaired, it was due for servicing, and Mr Allister was always most particular about that – put it in, regularly, once a month.'

'The car wasn't ready,' I said. 'Mrs Allister told me about it, when she visited me, on the afternoon of the accident. Mr Carmichael had dropped Mr Allister off at the garage that morning. Mr Allister said if the car wasn't ready he'd go by train. Mrs Allister was sure the garage wouldn't let her husband down.'

'Neither did we!' Shirley replied, with sudden indignation. 'The car was ready, all right! I remember seeing the work ticket, fastened under the windscreen wiper, when I got in at eight o'clock, and thinking I'd have to hurry to make out the invoice – we do the invoices from the mechanic's work ticket … I was checking it, when Mr Allister came in. Joe was in the office with me, and he told him the car was ready for him to drive away.'

I felt as though I had stopped breathing.

'Go on!' I said impatiently, to Shirley.

'Well, Joe and Mr Allister were talking about the weather, and Mr Allister said he'd heard the weather reports, and it was pretty sticky, he didn't like the idea of driving. He said he hated fog, and didn't fancy crawling all the way to town and back, so he told Joe to keep the car, and do some other little jobs he wanted fixed – something to do with the carburettor, I think. He arranged with Joe to bring the car to the station to meet the quarter to six train…'

'You're *sure* about this?' I said. 'Absolutely sure?'

'Of course I am!' Shirley retorted, with puzzled indignation. 'I was *there!* I heard all they said. Joe went to the station, and then he heard about the crash, so he drove it up to Mr Carmichael's place, and handed over the keys. All the trains were running *hours* late!'

'Who did he hand them to?' I asked.

'I don't know.' She was still looking puzzled, so I explained to her how much it would matter to Sally to know the truth. She offered to come down to the garage with me, at once.

Joe was there, at work on a car. Shirley told him all I had told her, and he repeated, almost word for word, the story that she had given me about Douglas.

'He wouldn't take the car,' Joe said. 'Said he didn't like the idea, with the weather so bad, and he'd been thinking about it, all the way to the garage. Said a train journey would be a change, anyway, and a bit of a rest for him.'

I asked him to whom he had given the car keys.

'Mr Carmichael's housekeeper. I told her that I'd been to the station and heard there was a crash and all the trains were delayed, so I'd brought the car, instead of waiting for him. I said I hoped Mr Allister wasn't on that train. Gosh, if I'd only *known*...'

I thanked Joe, and asked Shirley if I could use the office telephone; I phoned Miss Verney and said I wouldn't be able to come to tea, promising to explain next time I saw her ... and then I asked Joe to call me a taxi, to go to the House on the Hill.

All the way there, I kept thinking about it. In the confusion and unhappiness following the death of Douglas Allister, no one had thought to contact the garage, because it had simply been assumed that the car was not ready when Douglas called. And Shirley had not realised the importance of the conversation she had overheard because she did not know Sally was blaming herself for Douglas's train journey.

Mrs Hobson let me in, and the housekeeper told me that Mrs Allister did not want any visitors. I told her it was urgent, and went up the stairs as quickly as my weight would allow me. In the midst of my turbulent feelings, I remember wishing that this baby would hurry up and be born, because I was tried of carrying it around!

Sally was sitting in an armchair by her bedroom window, wan-faced, her usually pretty hair lank. She looked at me uninterestedly, as I came in and closed the door behind me.

'If you've come to do me good, I don't want it!' she said angrily.

'Sally Allister,' I said firmly, 'you're going to have that baby! You *aren't* going to lose it! It's Doug's baby, and you're not such a coward that you think you can back out of life the first time you're really up against things. All right, so I've never had to face your kind of sorrow and loneliness – perhaps I will one day! Maybe I'll feel bitter the way you do; for a time, anyway ... but I hope I won't run away from living!'

She said desolately:

'At least, you probably won't have to feel *responsible*, as well...'

'Neither will you, any longer!' I told her. And I repeated Shirley's story, and Joe's confirmation of it.

I shall always remember Sally's face as I talked. The frozen look went out of it. It was as though a great wind had shaken a tree with a storm of grief, and made the branches bend instead of breaking. The life came back and she began to cry – long, heart-breaking sobs, all the tears that had been dammed up for too long flowing freely at last. I went to her, and put my arms around her, saying nothing at all, because I had learnt the wisdom of silence.

She looked exhausted when she had no tears left to weep. She began to talk about Doug, how she had known him at kindergarten, how he had teased her during their school days, before he had gone away from Ambersea, how surprised and delighted she had been when he came back again.

I let her talk, while the shadows crept into the room. Finally, she said tiredly:

'Just think I might never have *known* if you hadn't seen Shirley!' She put a small, cold hand into mine. 'I don't feel that terrible sense of guilt any more. I just feel that fate is strange and cruel – Doug went by train because he thought it was safer.' She sighed. 'I know you're right, Julie – I'll live through this. It will take a long time, but one day...' She smiled wanly. 'Well, Father won't be lonely, with two children in the house. We shall stay here, now, of course ... and he'll have me to help him run the store again...'

I was crying, when David came in, just before evening surgery. He looked at me sharply, and I shook my head, managing a smile for him.

'Darling, this is just sheer reaction. I talked to Sally this afternoon...'

I told him the whole story. He listened with his arms around me, and they had never felt so comforting, such a refuge. When I had finished, he said gently:

'Thank heavens, Sally will be all right – in time. Sweetheart, you won't expect a quick miracle, will you? Sally is going to be lonely and unhappy for a very long time to come, but at least she has begun to come back to life again, and that's the important thing.'

I knew what he meant. Soon, there would be buds on the trees, and flowers in the gardens, but for Sally, this year, there would be no spring. All we could give her was patience and kindness and love...

'It doesn't seem right that we shall have so much happiness,' I whispered to David, and he answered me, with typical David-wisdom.

'Take happiness and be thankful for it, Julie; it's the most precious thing in life. Never spoil it by being fearful and feeling guilty about it. Sally had two lovely years. On her memories and her children, she will build a life again. And she will be happy again – because happiness, like the spring, *does* come again!'

I leant against him, feeling spent and yet at peace, hoping that the son or daughter we were soon to have would grow up to possess David's loving understanding, *his* most precious gift to *me*.

CHAPTER 12

Afterwards, looking back on that wild, mid-March day, I thought of it as a day on which the strangest things happened to me; although David insists that I attract odd happenings all the time, and says it must be due to something in my personal make-up!

David was away on a two-day medical conference. He hadn't wanted to leave me, and I had teased him about this.

'Darling, the baby isn't due for another two weeks yet! Mrs Charters will come in to clean; she'll be here all day, and Louise is spending the evening with me. The next day, Mrs Charters will be here again – and you're due home after tea.'

'You'll be alone one night,' he insisted unhappily.

'All right, if it makes you any happier, I'll ask Louise to stay overnight,' I said, touched by his concern. 'But honestly, there's nothing to worry about.'

'You're my wife, and it's our first baby,' he retorted, still not quite convinced that I should be perfectly safe while he was away for two days.

So he went off to his conference. He held me close, before he left, and said, without much conviction:

'Have a quiet time, darling!'

The first day passed quietly enough. Sally came to say goodbye to me. She was off to stay with friends in town, and was taking William with her. She looked bleak, and her smile did not reach her eyes, but she had begun her long journey along the quiet road of acceptance.

'I shall go to a show,' she said determinedly. 'Do some shopping; go to a couple of art exhibitions. Alun and Jane will thoroughly spoil William. I suppose it seems all wrong to be going to town and doing a lot of things. I ought to be spending a couple of weeks in the heart of the country, taking long walks, sorting myself out.'

'No,' I said gently. 'We each find our own solution to the problem of readjustment, Sally. And a couple of weeks of activity in town will do you good; there's so much going on, you'll be bound to take notice, and you won't have time to think too much; and we *can* think too much, sometimes.'

She gave me a quick, brief hug, and I said no more. One thing David had taught me well was the value of silence, especially in the face of grief such as Sally had known.

Mrs Charters came and cleaned and polished – and chatted about her six children. The last few weeks were always the worst, she assured me, and how I agreed with her! I felt large and unwieldy and found it difficult to imagine that I would ever again have a nice *flat* front!

Louise came at tea time. She had a heavy cold, and looked as though she was going to have influenza – there was an epidemic of it in Ambersea. She made valiant efforts to be her usual bright self, but seemed relieved when I suggested she should go early. I told David what I had done when he telephoned that evening, and he said worriedly.

'Julie, that means there's no one in the house with you…!'

'Darling, will you *please* stop worrying! All the doors are bolted and barred, I've got a tray of tea and a good book all ready to take to bed…'

'Any telephone calls?' he asked.

'One from Mother. She's looking forward to coming at the end of next week until after You-Know-Who is born! One from Clare … none for you! Sorry, darling!'

He laughed, and said:

'Well, Dr Paice is coping nicely with my

284

patients, I imagine. I wondered if there'd been any more anonymous calls?'

'No,' I assured him, and heard his sigh of relief.

There had been two such calls during the last week. Each time, the call had come after evening surgery, and David had taken it. A woman caller, he had told me; he had been troubled, because vaguely he knew that voice, somewhere. And each time the woman on the telephone had been agitated and distressed, asking him to come at once ... he had referred the caller to the doctor on the emergency list the first time, and on the second occasion David had been the doctor on call. In each case, the call had been a hoax, the people at the address given had known nothing about it...

'You should contact the police,' I had told him.

'I know.' He had hesitated. 'If it happens again, I shall *have* to; but I have a feeling about this ... I'm *sure* it's a patient of mine, though I can't place the voice. It's someone who needs help, not punishment.'

'If she needs help, she'll get it,' I pointed out. 'The law these days doesn't just punish; but people like you have to be protected from cranks. Supposing she called you out, and there was a *real* emergency for you while you were on a wild goose chase...?'

He had nodded, looking unhappy. I

285

understood his reluctance to go to the police, furious though I was with the anonymous caller – David, first and foremost a doctor, had a deep compassion for the darker side of human nature.

'Goodnight, my love,' he said, now. 'See you tomorrow. Take care...'

It was windy, and there were gusts of rain. It gave me a cosy feeling. The house and I were good friends, and I knew every creak and groan it gave in this kind of weather; but I missed David, as I snuggled beneath the blankets.

The morning brought fitful sunshine and sharp, strong gusts of wind. I watched the apple tree that grew close to the house, whose branches spread outside our sitting-room windows, and saw how wildly it tossed; it was an old tree, and had been planted when David's uncle was a boy.

David telephoned me soon after breakfast. He was annoyed that the conference, which he had expected would end at teatime, was going on into the evening, which meant he would be late home.

'Don't worry, darling,' I soothed him. 'I feel fine – bursting with energy, in fact.'

It was true. I felt I could have tackled all the spring-cleaning and finished it by teatime! Instead, I settled for turning out cupboards, and whisking around after dozens of overdue household tasks. Even

Mrs Charters commented on my energy.

'I was like that the day before my youngest was born,' she told me.

'I've got another two weeks to go yet! Nice if I feel energetic for that length of time!' I told her gaily.

The sun went to bed early, and it rained; the wind was rising, steadily increasing in violence, and I thought about the huge waves that would come crashing along the shore. I loved wild weather; it always reminded me, vividly, of the day I had watched David rescue a boy from the cliffs of Anchor Bay; on that day, I had finally known how much I loved David...

I could have walked for miles, I felt but, regretfully, I decided against going to the beach. Maybe it wouldn't be wise, in view of the sudden storms of rain and savage anger of the wind. Instead I settled for a brisk walk to Laura McCade's house; it was early closing day at the florists' where she worked, and I knew she would be at home.

Today, although she was pleased to see me, she seemed depressed.

'What's the matter?' I asked.

'Nothing, really,' she said, with a shame-faced air, pouring tea into the shallow, pretty cups. Then it came tumbling out, in a spate of words.

'I had a letter from my married niece, Jill. She suggests I should give up my home, and go and live with her and her husband. I don't want to; they're young, they'll have a family one of these days, and there isn't really room. Oh, it's kind of Jill, bless her! My eyesight isn't getting better, and I wonder, sometimes – what's the use of it all? Going on day after day, selling plants and flowers, coming back here to an empty house, going to bed, getting up next day ... getting a bit older, a bit slower. There should be more to life than that. When I was young, I was going to do so much. Now...' She shrugged, and sighed.

'I think we all feel this at some time or another in our lives,' I told Laura, and she nodded, saying with a sigh:

'It's different for you, Julie ... you have a husband, you're going to have a baby, a stake in the future. I haven't really minded not marrying, but I'd like to be *necessary* to someone.'

'That is everyone's need,' I told her. 'Look at Louise. She takes in students, spoils them, and gets enormous satisfaction out of knowing she's making a home for them while they're away from their own homes. You could do something like that...'

Laura shook her head and said nothing. I thought of the neat, lifeless rooms in her house. But we had discussed the question before and she was reluctant to have 'strangers' under her roof, as she put it.

288

I wanted to help her, but there was no easy solution to Laura's problem. I tried to cheer her up, but failed dismally, and I fretted about that fact all the way home.

The wind was in a furious rage, and I realised we were in for another wild night. The evening paper reported storm damage throughout the country and I worried about David, driving home late. As I pulled the curtains together I saw the frenzied dance of the apple-tree; it looked as though it would pull free of earth and fly away on the next made gust of wind.

My own fierce storm of energy had worn itself out. I had done too much, I thought, and the walk to and from Laura's had been a long one. I had been aware of a small thrust of pain in my back as I sat talking to her; there was the pain again, as I reached up to draw the curtains. Well, I thought, I shall have a leisurely evening, waiting for David. He expected to arrive about nine o'clock...

I was restless and could not read. The violence of the wind frightened me, for it seemed as though it would strip the roof from the solid old house. When I felt the pain again, I thought, suspicious and yet incredulous: but this can't *possibly* be...! Nevertheless, I looked at the clock, and made a mental note of the time...

And then, some time later came the

telephone call that, temporarily, drove all other thoughts from my head.

I lifted the receiver, expecting to hear David's voice, telling me that the storm had delayed him; but it was a woman's voice, high and sharp and breathless.

'Ask Dr Pembury to come at once, please...? At *once*...! Number Seven Halesworth Crescent... It's extremely urgent ... it's my next-door neighbour – she's going to have a baby and something's gone terribly wrong ... tell the doctor to *hurry*...! I don't know what to do...!'

I was about to tell her that David was away, and Dr Piper was on emergency call that evening, when, suddenly, there was an angry whistling in my ear, and the line went dead. I pressed the centre of the receiver up and down for several seconds, in vain; there was no reassuring purr of sound. The storm! I thought helplessly. The telephone lines were down, and somewhere a frantic woman was trying to contact a doctor. Somewhere, I had heard that voice before, and, though I have a good memory for voices, I couldn't place it.

I certainly was not my usual calm, sensible self that evening, as I often tell David. Had I been, I would have realised at once that the caller would probably ring again, and, getting no reply, call another doctor. Confused and uncertain, I imagined her wondering what had happened; anyway, I ought to report that our telephone was out of order...

I pulled on a coat, and wound a scarf around my head; there was a telephone in the house next door – but Mrs Jekins, who lived there, was wintering in the sunshine of Malta. The people who lived on the other side of us were giving a party, and I hesitated to disturb them. There were our neighbours across the road, but it was just as easy to save explanations and walk to the telephone box at the end of the road. I decided; it was less than five minutes' walk away.

The wind seemed to be trying to push me back indoors. I bent my head against it, and fought my way to the end of the road... Grimly, I battled towards the glass-sided booth ... I could hear the crash of tiles in the distance, and small tree branches were swept wildly along the centre of the road.

There was someone in the telephone box. A slim woman in a mackintosh, angrily tapping the centre of the receiver rest with impatient fingers. As I reached the booth, she almost flung the receiver back, and turned, opening the door so quickly that she all but sent it crashing into me.

The angry protests died in my lips as I saw her face. She was in her forties, with hard eyes and mouth, her make-up applied with a heavy hand, her hair an impossibly bright gold beneath the head-scarf.

She looked startled and momentarily uneasy, at seeing me there. I suppose that, being so very pregnant, I must have looked too vast to be easily thrust out of the way! But as she glared at me, I knew where I had seen her before, and the first missing piece of the jigsaw fell neatly into place.

My memory reached back to an evening just before Christmas; a hard-faced, smartly dressed woman at the door, just as David was finishing evening surgery; no, she admitted coolly, she wasn't one of David's patients. She wished to see him as a *private* patient, and it was most urgent; she had to see him this evening.

I had admitted her reluctantly; it had been a long, hard day for David and I knew he was tired – but I would never turn anyone away from a doctor's door.

David was with her in his surgery for some time. I heard her leave, and when he joined me for our evening meal, he spoke to me wrathfully about his blonde visitor.

'Of all the *impudence!* She's cashier at the Fig Tree and her husband has been away in the Merchant Navy for the last five months – he's due home next month. She's two months pregnant by a "man friend", as she puts it – and wants me to do something about it, before her husband comes home! She calmly suggested that she was sure I could, or that I'd put her in touch with someone ... what on earth does she think doctors are here for, I wonder? I could understand an irresponsible teenager making such a request – but a woman of *her* age, in her forties...! Good heavens! I told her a few home truths, and she went away with an outraged air of being refused something to which she was entitled...!'

David had said a good deal more in the same vein. I listened and sympathised, sharing his indignation. And now the woman who had stormed out of the surgery that night, faced me in the telephone box. I could see at once that she was no longer pregnant; but there were shadows under her heavily mascaraed eyes, and her face was drawn.

She tried to push past me, suddenly avoiding my long look.

'Telephone's out of order,' she said; and the second piece of the jigsaw puzzle clicked into position. It was the same voice that had spoken to me, moments ago, before the line went dead.

I thought, for a moment, that it was an incredible coincidence. Later, I realised that it was not such a coincidence, after all. That was when I discovered that she lived not fifteen minutes' walk from David's surgery and had several telephone boxes to choose from, in the vicinity, from which to make her calls.

'*You* telephoned just now!' I cried. 'I remember your voice ... but you said "Halesworth Crescent"! That's the other side of Ambersea, more than half an hour's journey by bus! I'm Dr Pembury's wife and I took the call ... I don't understand...!'

But I did understand – all at once. Perhaps my senses were sharpened, suddenly, as I stood there, in the furious storm, looking at her, calculating that it had not taken me long to get to the telephone box, and she, disappointed, had lingered there unwisely, frustrated that her call had misfired, determined to try again ... she was the anonymous caller, deliberately harassing David because of her anger that he had not given her help to which she considered she was entitled!

She glared at me. In the brightness of her eyes, the unwaving blankness of her look, I recognised the tilting of a delicate balance between reason and the wild chaos of emotion that leads to mental illness.

'I know you,' I said. 'I know why you came to the surgery!'

'You had no right to know that!' she cried.

'A doctor has the right to discuss his patients with his wife – if he knows his confidences are respected!' I retorted. '*You've* been phoning David, sending him out on fictitious errands, at the end of a tough day dealing with people who *really* need his services! He should report you to the police, but he feels sorry for you, though he doesn't realise who you are! I see now why you do this to him ... a very subtle revenge – a fake maternity call!'

'You can't prove anything!' she cried. Her too-bright eyes swept contemptuously over my bulky figure. 'So *you're* having a baby! That's fine, isn't it? Really funny! Life's easy and tidy for people like you, the sort who never make mistakes!'

'Plenty of women make your kind of mistake!' I retorted frankly. 'Neither David nor I condemn! "There but for the grace of God go I..." It's not facing up to it that's so wrong. Expecting someone to find the easy way out, instead of having the courage to see it through! Asking a doctor to do something contrary to all his teaching, his principles ... deliberately harassing him out of spite, because he couldn't and wouldn't help you back out...!'

'Oh, keep your sermon!' she shouted, above the voice of the wind. 'People like you and your husband make me sick!' She began to laugh hysterically, looking down at her slim figure. 'I lost the baby, anyway... My husband came home and we had a terrible scene ... now he's left me...'

She thrust me violently aside. Just for a moment, I saw the agony in her face, and felt terribly sorry for her. Involuntarily, I put out a hand, but she was gone into the darkness, a slight figure in a tightly-belted mackintosh, running back to a lonely flat, somewhere... I knew she wouldn't trouble David again, just as I knew she needed help...

There was nothing I could do; a terrible weariness washed over me. The pain came back, insistent, as though demanding why I had ignored its message ... the thought of struggling back through the gale was almost too much, but I had to. I must go to the house across the road from us, I decided, and ask them to telephone the maternity home ... maybe their phone was out of order, too.

I had to stop twice on the way. What a long road it was! Once, as I stood, fighting for breath, feeling suddenly and inexplicably panic-stricken, I thought I heard a crash like thunder and the splintering sound of broken glass... I just wanted to get home, and my feet seemed weighted.

I was almost there when I was aware of a sudden commotion ... more lights on than usual in the houses around ours, people coming out into the street, somebody calling that the police had been told – and then, as I paused beneath the street lamp near the gate, I realised two things simultaneously: that the commotion was centred on our house, and that Laura, of all people, was running towards me, crying frantically:

'Julie! *Julie.* Oh, you're all right, thank heavens! You weren't there...!'

'What's the matter?' I demanded. 'What's happening?'

'I arrived just as it happened!' she said. 'I was at the gate, when I heard this tremendous noise at the back of the house. There's a tree down and it's crashed through the living-room; I thought you were there – you'd have been badly hurt...!'

She was right, as I afterwards discovered. The apple-tree had finally yielded to the storm, falling across the little terrace where David and I sat in summer, its upper branches crashing through the french doors to the living-room, sending glass flying in all directions, wrenching away the doors themselves, and creating havoc everywhere. Plaster had come down from the ceiling, the electric light fitting had been torn. By a miracle, there was no fire, for David's Christmas present to the house had been the installation of central heating; but I should certainly have been seriously cut by flying glass and injured by falling plaster had I still been in the room.

They say that, in a split second, a drowning man reviews all the events of his life, like a film reel unrolled in front of him; in an equally short space of time, I reviewed, astonished, the strange events of an extraordinary day – the day on which my baby was going to be born.

I thought of my morning visit from Sally, who was facing the future with courage; of Laura, who had been my first patient in Ambersea, here by my side now; and finally, of the crazy twist of fate that I should have been saved from injury by a woman who had revenged herself on my husband! Had she not telephoned, I would have had no reason to leave the house when I did. I kept thinking that life was strange and fantastic and never would make sense ... the woman whose name I did not yet know never dreamed that her action would save me from serious harm! One day soon, I thought, I'm going to find out who she is and where she lives – that won't be difficult; I'm going to tell her what happened tonight and try to persuade her to accept the help that she needs ... it will be my first task when this other, more important one, is over.

'Laura,' I said, surprised at the calmness of my voice, 'I think we should contact the maternity home, and then see if we can get a taxi. This baby has decided to arrive two weeks early; I wish David had been here!'

It was the one thing that flawed my pleasure and anticipation as we drove towards the hospital, with Laura sitting calmly beside me; she had been amazingly brisk and competent, taking charge of the situation, getting me into the taxi. I asked her why she had called, and she said wryly:

'I felt guilty that I'd loaded my troubles on you at such a time, my conscience bothered me, so I decided to come and apologise. No one has any right, these days, to wallow in self-pity. I ought to be ashamed of myself! I'm going to stay here in Ambersea, and keep my independence. There are plenty of things I can do ... to start with, I can take a leaf from Louise's book, and let one of those empty rooms to someone who needs comfort and quiet, instead of dusting them every day and then closing the door on them, as though they were *shrines!*'

I reached for her hand and patted it. Dear Laura, I thought, with her sound common sense and courage, would, like Sally, find her own solution to her problems; and I was glad, because already she sounded happier.

I thought I should remember clearly every moment of the night on which our baby was born, but, looking back, I find that the edges are blurred, even now ... I remember the nurse, brisk and kind, helping me to undress, saying that it would be some little while yet, and she'd look in after her supperbreak to see how I was getting on ... there was a bell, if I needed it ... I remember thinking that my mother was going to feel cheated, and then wishing again, rather forlornly, that David could have been back in time to be with me... Then I thought once again of the strange quirks of fate.

And then the pains were sharper, more urgent ... until they took me away to a clean, quiet room that smelt of antiseptic, and when the pain was too demanding I could breathe deeply, under the kindly guidance of the nurse, into the magic little black object that sent me sailing on rosy clouds, for a little while...

The two most wonderful moments of all came almost simultaneously. First, the nurse saying happily:

'Your husband has just arrived, Mrs Pembury!'

And then, before I had time to savour the delight of David being with me, just in time, came that great moment of birth ... the second of heart-stopping fear, and *waiting,* then the thin, furious wail of an indignant baby thrust out into the world.

'It's a boy!' the doctor told me. 'An eight-pound boy, Mrs Pembury! Perfect! And with a good pair of lungs!'

It seemed so long before I was finally allowed back in bed in the small room that David had booked, weeks ago, for me. It was eternity before the smiling nurse brought me a cup of tea, fussed with the bedclothes, told me I could have both my son and my husband in a few seconds, and whisked away with the familiar starched-apron rustle that reminded me of my first day as district nurse.

They put the baby into my arms seconds before they let David into the room. A newborn baby is not beautiful, I know, but the child we had decided to call Michael David, if it was a boy, was, at that moment, the most beautiful person in the world to me. I wept. The nurse would have said it was reaction, but I knew better – it was with pride and joy for this, the strangest and loveliest day of my life, and the gift it had given.

David almost exploded into the room. He looked dishevelled and frantic, and scarcely looked at the baby! He kissed me, then straightened, and demanded wrathfully:

'Julie, what on *earth* is going on? I come home to find the house in an uproar, and you having a baby two weeks early! And Laura McCade tells me some garbled story about you being out of doors, by a miracle, when the tree collapsed ... what do you think you're doing!'

'Just having a baby, darling!' I told him meekly. 'I'll tell you the whole story later. It's quite an astonishing tale!'

'I might have known that not even having a baby would be straightforward and uneventful for *you!*' he retorted, distractedly, running a hand through his hair.

'It's your baby, too, remember!' I told him.

'You talk as though his mother is a witch!'

'So she is!' He smiled, suddenly, looking at us both with pride, tenderness and amusement.

'A witch!' he affirmed solemnly, bending to kiss me again. 'She attracts all kinds of happenings! She can't help it! Poor little boy, let's hope he has inherited his father's splendid qualities, his sound, practical nature and good common sense!'

I laughed, putting up my free hand to draw his face close to mine.

'Some time, darling,' I said calmly, 'remind me to enlighten you about a few things concerned with Michael's father having common sense and a practical nature!'

'I love you!' he said.

'I love you, too!' I told him.

This Large Print Book, for people who cannot read normal print, is published under the auspices of

THE ULVERSCROFT FOUNDATION